A TOR DOUBLE

ACTION WESTERN

D1571064

**Look for Tor Double Action Westerns
Coming soon from these authors**

MAX BRAND

ZANE GREY

LEWIS B. PATTEN

WAYNE D. OVERHOLSER

CLAY FISHER

FRANK BONHAM

OWEN WISTER

STEVE FRAZEE

HARRY SINCLAIR DRAGO

JOHN PRESCOTT

WILL HENRY

Frank Bonham

THAT BLOODY
BOZEMAN TRAIL

STAGECOACH WEST!

TOR®

A TOM DOHERTY ASSOCIATES BOOK
NEW YORK

THAT BLOODY BOZEMAN TRAIL

Copyright © 1950 by Popular Publications, Inc. First published in *Dime Western*. Reprinted by permission of the author and Mrs. Gloria Bonham.

STAGECOACH WEST!

Copyright © 1950 by Popular Publications, Inc. First published in *Dime Western*. Reprinted by permission of the author and Mrs. Gloria Bonham.

Copyright © 1990 by Tor Books

A Tor Book
Published by Tom Doherty Associates, Inc.
49 West 24th Street
New York, N.Y. 10010

Cover art by Bernal

ISBN: 0-812-50534-4

First edition: July 1990

Printed in the United States of America

0 9 8 7 6 5 4 3 2 1

THAT BLOODY
BOZEMAN TRAIL

1

Too Tough for the Army

SAM CARY LEFT THE INTERIOR OF THE YELLOW RAIL-
road station and paused a moment in the doorway
before stepping into the sunlight. He was tall and
limber-muscled, wearing a softly-tanned leather shirt
and old cavalry breeches with stripes of darker blue
where the yellow slashes had been removed. His flat
Stetson was worn forward and to one side, a hat with
its own casualness, the color of the deserts.

Glancing about him, he breathed the hot smell of the
prairie town. Before him, the steel tracks glistened under the sun. A handcar was drawn up beside the ties
and at the corner of the station an Indian pony scratched
luxuriously against a wooden sign nailed to the building. Cary's glance went briefly beyond it, to his own
wagon camp a short distance away. A man on horse-
back rode into the sprawling square of wagons, dragging a load of mesquite roots by a rope. Bullwhackers
worked stolidly in the morning heat, putting down the

last of the freight for the haul from this railroad town
of Cheyenne to Cary's trading post on the Montana border.

Cary turned to watch two of his teamsters back-and-
bellying a crate from the loading dock, noting that four
barrels still remained. Again he glanced at the camp,
saw no one coming for the barrels and stepped into the
sunlight and crossed the tracks. Vaulting up on the high
dock, he frowned at the words he had chalked on the
tops of the barrels.

DONOVAN—REPACK.

Looking up, he saw his wagonmaster, John Silvertooth, coming from the camp. Cary dropped to the
ground and walked to meet him. The scorch of heated
earth went through his bootsoles. The sun was like yellow glass melting in the sky. The thick, blackstrap odor
of sage was in the air. Reaching Silvertooth, Cary asked
off-handedly, ''Where's Donovan?''

Silvertooth took time to fill his pipe. He was a big
man in a red miner's shirt and smoke-tanned buckskin
trousers. Deep grooves of displeasure pinched the skin
between his eyes.

''Ain't seen him since breakfast,'' he said. ''I hear it
took six men to put him out of The Nations last night.
If he's got a hangover the size of his drunk, he'll sweat
boilermakers for a week.''

They walked toward camp. At the forge-wagon, a
shirtless workman struck a rosy ox-shoe with ringing
echoes.

Sam Cary stopped in the shade of a tall freight wagon.
There was no sign of activity at Donovan's faded blue
Murphy wagon. Crates and barrels stood about and the
tail-gate was down. Cary took a long breath of dissatisfaction.

Silvertooth heard it and spat a mouthful of smoke.

"I say he's a troublemaker by trade. I could find a dozen better than him in any saloon."

"Soberer, maybe," Cary agreed. "But oxen and Ogallalas don't set much store by whether or not a man's taken the pledge. Once we leave town, he won't be finding a saloon at every corner."

"*If* we leave town," said the wagonmaster.

"We always have, haven't we?"

"Up to now. But these bullwhackers are spoiling faster than pork and the pork smells to high heaven. They had an edge like a Green River knife a week ago. They'd had their fun and were set to go. Now they've lost it."

Cary leaned by one elbow against a wheel a foot taller than he was. "They'll get it back fast enough, once they're standing night guard in Sioux country."

Disgruntlement did not leave Silvertooth's eyes. "Not with an Irishman like Donovan bragging of what he's getting away with. Castro come to me this morning and asked could he pay back his advance and go out with Mark Stockwell's outfit. Stockwell got here three days after us, and he's going out before."

"What did you tell him?"

Silvertooth glanced at a cut knuckle. "I told him, no. There won't any more of them ask it, but I don't like the look of it. That Mick put him up to it. The same as he came to you and offered to sign on if you'd loan him the money to buy out of the army."

"Still a bargain," Cary stated. "He can't stand freedom. That's all that ails Donovan. Once we stretch out, he'll pay his way."

"I don't like gambling on whackers. Not this year. This is the Sioux's year. The year of the big hunt. We should have gone out a week ago, when the men were standing on their hind legs clawing at the sky."

Carey smiled. "Don't blame me. I only own half this outfit. The other half will be here tomorrow sure—if the train doesn't get stampeded by a herd of buffalo."

He found a dipper on a nail and raised the lid of a

barrel lashed to the side of the wagon. Pouring a dip-
perful in his hat, he set it on the ground to soak. It slid
tepidly over his chest and puddled above his belt. Then
he poured the water out of his hat and glanced up to
see Silvertooth frowning at him.

"Are you going to let Gaybird go with us?"

For a moment Cary's mouth got tight. He regarded
the other man flatly. "What have I got to say about it?
She's of age."

"She's your ward, ain't she?"

"At eighteen? She can sign checks now, and pick a
husband. She'll be making her own decisions." He
frowned. "Though of course I mean to throw the fear
into her about the trail."

"I'd think so," said Silvertooth pompously. "If I
was you, I'd say to her, 'Look here! That Bozeman road
ain't no doings for a white man any more, let alone a
woman. You get on that train tomorrow and go back to
Cincinnati!' Though I don't expect she'll be fighting to
live in a wagon anyhow, after the seminary."

Cary smiled. "You're talking about handling squaws
and horses, John. Gaybird isn't quite either. She's cold-
jawed as a bronc and smart as a young squaw. She'll
want to be handled cleverly."

Carefully he set his hat over his eye. They left the
shade of the wagon.

"I thought of buying her out," he explained. "Her
dad's half-interest ought to be worth fifteen thousand by
now. I could give notes."

"She couldn't live on notes."

"I've got some cash."

"None you don't need. You owe Bill Orrum two
thousand on those rifles." Then he looked startled and
glanced about to be sure no one had followed, trade
arms being banned on the Bozeman road this year. He
referred to the code word, more loudly than was nec-
essary. "I say, you need two thousand to pay for that
hardware."

"God forbid I should ever need you for a spy," Cary chuckled. "I could give her some cash now and a thousand or so at the end of the summer. It's not right she should go into that Indian warren again. That was all right for her dad, and for a girl of thirteen. It was peaceful, then; part of the time, anyway. But she's no child, now. She'd find it rough."

Silvertooth tapped the hot, gray tobacco with his thumb. "She didn't find it rough last time she was out. She was riding everything in the corral. She learned to talk Ogallala with the washwomen."

"That," Cary pointed out, "was summer before last. She was sixteen. There's a difference between a girl of sixteen and one of eighteen."

Silvertooth thought, and nodded, and said, "Yes, I reckon there is."

Cary had the nostalgic feeling that he would never see her again, the curious, laughing little girl-animal with black pigtails whom Old Bob Phillips had left him to raise five years ago. A freighting accident had ended Cary and Phillips' partnership in Fort Graybull a year after they built it. Cary had installed the girl in a seminary in Cincinnati; summers, she visited the post.

On her last visit, two years ago, she had been a fascinating half-civilized creature of sixteen. But Indian smokes had fumed too steadily last summer, and he had instructed her not to come out. He had again advised it this spring, but now it was June and he had her letter saying she would be out, and please wait for her in Cheyenne when he made up his annual freight-train.

He would wait, of course; but she could not make him take her. A man must go by his judgment, and Sam Cary himself was returning to the Bighorn country only because his trade forced him to.

They crossed the camp through the jungle of trash, tarpaulins and tarbuckets to Donovan's wagon-and-trailer outfit. Silvertooth looked about. He said bitterly, "Look at that!"

In the slovenliness of the wagon there was offense to a wagon-master. The tailgate slouched against a wheel and crates sat about in total lack of order. A rack of lead-lined yokes was overturned by the wagon. Silvertooth's hand angrily swept a heap of pipe dottle from the wagon-bed.

"Damned if he ain't trying to burn the outfit up, now!"

Cary recalled a conversation with Tom Braga, who ran The Nations saloon. He said thoughtfully, "Braga was talking about a shotgun the other day. Donovan had been raising a little hell the night before. Pig-knuckles brine all over the nude behind the bar. A shame, at that. Braga was fond of that picture, and now the lady's left breast has run."

Silvertooth squinted with a tart blue eye. "A shotgun, eh? On one of our boys?"

Cary shrugged. "Talk. Donovan didn't have any money, did he?" His glance went curiously to Silvertooth.

Color invaded Silvertooth's face. "Not honest-to-God money, I reckon. I gave him four-bits for a pick-me-up after breakfast. He was shaking like a Cheyenne pup in February. But on four-bits he couldn't raise a smile."

Cary regarded him frowningly and began to walk back toward the tracks. After a moment Silvertooth followed. "Listen," he said, "he couldn't get in trouble on four-bits."

"After last night he could get in trouble by just showing his Irish face in The Nations."

"He knows better than that. . . . Don't he?" Silvertooth demanded.

"Maybeso. I keep thinking about that nude."

They reached the tracks and gazed up the dusty main street. Horses, turnouts and pedestrians briskly came and went through the rutted avenue cutting across the casual sprawl of tents, frame buildings and brick structures. "Well, we'll take a look," Cary said.

They crossed the tracks and passed the big trail outfit from Fort Stockwell, Montana Territory—Mark Stockwell's trading post in the Gallatin Valley. With dissatisfaction, Cary noted that a number of Stockwell's wagons were sheeted and ready to move. And they'd arrived after Cary.

Silvertooth observed this, also, and commented sourly, "He's worked the tallow out of his boys to hit the road ahead of us. If he takes out first, we'll live in his dust and camp trash and drink the brine he leaves in the waterholes all the way back to the border."

"Maybe his mules will all come down with the swinney," Cary said. "Not that I wish him bad luck."

They moved into town. Cary kept to the thin slice of shade against the buildings. The sun, reflecting from the bleached ground, pinched his eyes. Freight outfits whooped and lurched along the shallow canyon of the street. Railroad workers were everywhere, hard-bitten Irishmen on their way to end-of-track or heading back from it. Soldiers from Fort Russell sauntered about. Distantly a smith's sledge shaped a tire to a wheel bound for the wilderness.

This was still a town of primary colors and emotions, running more to tent and frame than to brick, more to fights than discussions.

In this vigorous emotional climate, gunsmiths outthrove haberdashers, and saloonkeepers prospered above all others. Donovan might be in any of twenty saloons, spending his fifty cents on beer or hunting whiskey credit. They glanced into the Shamrock, but the bullwhacker's bearish shoulders were not at the bar. They tried the Copperopolis. Donovan had not been seen.

Moving on, they investigated the Pawnee Bar. The Irishman was not at the bar, but as they went out the door a lean, dark-skinned man in stained buckskins collided with them. He wore a round-crowned Stetson, from which pigtails descended, tied with greasy rawhide bows. Cary stared past him but the newcomer said with a grin, "Howdy, Cary! Are you early or am I late?"

Cary said, "We're both early. I'll see you later, Orrum. In front of Bailey's."

Bill Orrum saluted and stood aside, a tall and indolent man with a fondness for rings and Indian tobacco. Silvertooth did not hide his dislike for the man as they passed; he failed to speak, and after they were on the walk he growled at Cary, "You're not parading around with that offscraping right in the open, are you?"

"He's got guns," Cary said shortly. "If the army won't let us buy them openly, we'll buy them in back lots and carry them under bolts of cloth. I don't know whether they're more afraid of the guns falling into the hands of Indians, or of honest traders making a dollar. We aren't going back into the Sioux country with the kind of blunderbusses the whackers are carrying."

Silvertooth grunted. "The smell of him will rub off onto you if anybody sees you talking to him. He ain't going up the Bozeman with us, is he?"

"No. I take delivery of the guns in the brush."

They had drinks at the Shamrock, after failing to locate Donovan in any of the larger bars. He had not been at The Nations, and Cary found the edge of his concern dulling. Afterward, Silvertooth went up the street on business of his own. Cary consulted his watch. It was time now for his meeting with Bill Orrum. Yet he did not hurry. He had another drink, wanting savagely to persuade Orrum that they had nothing in common beyond a mutual interest in contraband weapons. Orrum was a shotgun trader; a smuggler of whiskey into Indian territory, and the operator of a sporting house in Bannock. It was a demeaning thing to trade with him, but necessity had shaped many a man's ethics before Cary's.

In front of Bailey's Hardware, a collection of crates partially blocked the board sidewalk. Bill Orrum's crowlike shape was balanced on a crate as Cary approached. He was in conversation with another man. Cary hesitated. It would not do to seem to have an appointment with him: Orrum's trade was too well-known. The army was lackadaisically inspecting all wagons going north on the Bozeman, but friends of Orrum's ran the risk of a more careful inspection.

Orrum's round-crowned Stetson hung between his shoulder blades by the rawhide lanyard. His black braids glistened with grease. His head obscured the face of the other man, so that Cary had approached to within twenty feet when the trader leaned back, exposing the face of Mark Stockwell.

Cary's inclination was to pass them up. But Orrum glanced around at a word from Stockwell, and his deep, slow voice said, "You've kept me waiting."

Cary put a bootsole against a crate, a dry disgust in his eyes. "Well, you see I was up with a sick teamster," he said. "You seem to be in good company, anyhow."

Orrum smoked a red India pipe and regarded Cary lazily. Smoking enough *shongsasha* in time wrapped a man in an aura of wildness, as his buckskins took on the wilderness stain of buffalo grease and woodsmoke. Orrum had acquired this fragrance. He wore Blackfoot moccasins and was sombre and sparing of humor.

"I could teach you things about freighting," he remarked. "One of them is not to hire a crew till you're ready to stretch. Whackers spoil faster than venison once they've taken the notion to travel. I hear your outfit's falling apart."

Mark Stockwell's pottery-brown eyes smiled. "Sam's in no condition to travel anyway, Bill. He's expecting. Every year about this time he becomes a father for the summer. He's got a black-haired ward with a waist you could span with your two hands.''

He laughed and punched Cary. Big and heavy-boned, durable as a Murphy wagon, Stockwell had a rugged countenance with a strong ledge of bone over his eyes. His shoulders filled his brown blanket-coat and his neck was short and strong.

"When's she coming in?" Orrum asked carelessly.

"Tomorrow."

"Is she going up to the fort with you?" Stockwell demanded.

"Hard to say."

"If she were *my* ward, it wouldn't be hard. The Sioux are hunting early, like they had a big show planned for fall. We didn't lose sight of their smoke till we left the Bighorns.''

Orrum sipped smoke from the pipe. "I reckon you boys could cut some throats in Washington for abandoning the Bozeman posts, ey?''

Stockwell shrugged. "They were blunderers; but they might have blundered in some time when we wanted them. Still—I keep the Injuns buttered up.''

Cary regarded him quietly. "With ninety proof butter? You're new to the Nations, Mark. I don't know how it was with you in New Mexico, but up here a man who buys the Indians' friendship with whiskey is chiseling his own headstone. When you take it away from them, you'll have a chivaree on your hands.''

Stockwell smiled. "Maybe I won't take it away from them. I tease them: A bottle now, a bottle then. It gets me bargains when they come to trade. And I see to it that they do their drinking away from the post.''

Orrum exhaled a grayness of bitter smoke. "I wonder how-come the army to pull out? They lost a hundred and fifty men holding the posts last summer. Then they pulled out. Does that make sense?''

"Why do they wear winter uniforms until the men drop from the heat?" Cary said. "Because the head of the brute is in Washington, and the tail's in Wyoming. They'll let a trader build his post in the Sioux country on the proposition that he'll have protection. Then they walk out on him, and the trade dries up. Mark and I are the army, this season."

Black as currants, Orrum's eyes crinkled. "Or you might say you are, Sam. Mark had the good sense to build in Montana."

Stockwell's good-humor thinned to a pinch at the corners of his mouth. "Don't hold it against me that the army pulled out on you," he said. "You talked it around that I was a fool to build my post where I did. You thought you'd grab off all the trade bound for the Montana mines before it ever reached me. For a while, you nearly did. The point is, I saw the time coming when the army would pull out and the travel would steer away from the Bozeman. The Bighorns have been Sioux country for centuries. It's the last big hunting ground, and you know and I know and the army knows that they won't give it up without a scrap. So the army gave up."

With a gold cigar-cutter, he trimmed a cigar. He roasted it in a match-flame, and when Cary said nothing, merely watching him with a curious, half-amused light in his eyes, he said, "So now the traffic goes north and east of us, by Missouri River packet. But they still come down from the mines to trade with Mark Stockwell. The lesson in it is—never trust the army."

"Isn't that the lesson for both of us?" Cary pointed out. "When they man the forts again, you'll be swapping trade beads to squaws for coyote pelts. Just when you expect the army least, they'll come back."

Stockwell said drily, "Let's all hope they come back. There's room for both of us. We can be rivals, can't we, without being enemies?"

"I've always thought so," Cary smiled.

The trader made a place for himself on the walk, moving unhurriedly toward the foot of town.

Cary then stared quickly and without rancor at Bill Orrum.

"We'll come to that," Orrum said. "Walk up to my camp with me." Sam watched him strike his pipe against a crate. He's more like an Indian than Crazy Dog himself, Sam thought. He's got the wild smell, the pigtails, the dark and greasy look.

Orrum's way was to bring in ten or fifteen wagons loaded with what he could sell quickly, dispose of it along with the wagons, and leave himself encumbered only with gold. His camp was in a coulee west of town, and consisted of a bedroll, a deerhide tent, one wagon, three span of oxen and a riding mule. He had jerked venison drying on a line, and yanked off a strip and tossed it to Cary. Cary held it but did not eat: it was easier to tell a man he was a liar and a thief than to say his food was filthy.

From the tent, Orrum procured a rifle. He drew it and laid his cheek against the stock, sighting briefly and letting the hammer *snick*. "Springfield-Allin," he said. "Trapdoor Springfield."

It had a grand balance in Cary's hands. It was snug and compact, and so new the grease had not all been rubbed off. He sighted and let the hammer drop. Quickly he re-cocked and threw open the trapdoor breech. The gun was at his cheek again in three seconds.

"This is the one," he breathed. His hand rubbed the brass lock-plate.

"One hundred Springfield-Allins," said Orrum, chewing the jerky. "Same price, forty dollars apiece, cash. Four thousand . . ."

Cary's eyes snapped. "*Half* cash! The rest at the end of the season. That was the bargain."

Orrum shrugged. "That was before we knew how bad things was. When they massacred them miners last month I got to thinking all cash might be a better idea.

I hear, too, they put an arrow in John Silvertooth's rump at Old Woman Creek on your way down.''

"Did you, now?'' Cary said.

Orrum recovered the gun. Putting it back in the tent, he said, "No matter, Sam. I can sell 'em.''

Cary's hand pulled him around and there was a meaty slap as his palm wiped across the gun-runner's cheek. "You're not going to hedge on me! I had the money brought up from Denver, but half of it goes into supplies.''

Orrum's eyes snapped blackly as he stood under the pressure of Cary's hand. "I owe every dollar I'll get out of this to the bank. I can get the cash from somebody else if I can't from you. I'm traveling north with Stockwell. I reckon he'd buy them in a minute.''

"How much,'' Cary asked, "is he paying you to hold me up?''

"You wouldn't think much of me if I told my customers' names, would you, Sam?'' Orrum smiled.

"I don't think much of you—put it that way. Where are the guns?''

Orrum grinned. "Where's the four thousand?'' He turned away to build a fire under a kettle. "I'll be around the Nations till ten o'clock. After that, I don't know where I'll be. But somebody else will have the map of where I left the guns.''

Cary pulled a buckskin whang from the yoke of his shirt. His hands tugged on it a moment before it snapped. He threw the pieces in the fire. He said, "I'll draw the money out of the bank today and leave it at The Nations. Where's the map of your cache?''

Orrum grinned, and from his shirt he pulled a small patch of rawhide. On it he had drawn a map of where the guns were hidden. "They're in Sweetwater Coulee,'' he said. "Oxen chained to the wheels. A night's drive in, but start early if you want to beat the sun.''

Cary put the rawhide inside his own shirt. "Thanks,'' he said, and his shoulder moved and Orrum ducked too late. The fist cracked against his cheekbone. He stumbled against his tent and fell. He lay there with his black eyes dull and evil as those of a sand rattler. He said, "I'll remember that."

Cary's shoulders moved. "Fine. Now we've both got something to remember."

It was mid-afternoon when he sauntered down the street, but it had not cooled. The heat made a man think of liquids. Cary let his glance travel downstreet. A burly figure in a red shirt approached through the turmoil of boardwalk traffic, moving quickly, and Cary suddenly saw that it was his wagonmaster.

"One of the whackers just came in," Silvertooth said. "He says Donovan tried to borrow money from him."

"Did he let him have it?"

"No. But Donovan said he was going to have his liquor at The Nations or wreck the place. He's down the street."

Cary frowningly hitched up his belt. Both men stopped across the street from the big false-fronted saloon. In the stifling afternoon, horses crowded the unbarked hitch racks. Now a great-shouldered shape of a man lounged from the foot of town and stopped before the slotted doors of the saloon. The sun burned in Donovan's crisp red hair. Cary saw him glance down at his palm, toss a coin on it and with resolution move into the saloon.

"The crazy Mick!" Silvertooth breathed.

Cary called out, but the doors had closed behind the freighter. They crossed the street. Cary stroked the slotted doors aside and glanced into the saloon. There was a feeling of lassitude in the huge, rough room with its mud walls and blackiron chandeliers. Customers were plentiful, but it was early for celebrating. Dice bounced, cards flashed, a soprano voice shrill with whiskey was singing, *Oh Willie, We Have Missed You.* Behind the bar was Braga's notorious nude, an opulent lithograph of a naked woman recumbent on a field of leopard skin. Brine of pig's knuckles had smeared her bosom.

Donovan was moving along the bar, his figure wreathed in tobacco fumes. He was a black Irishman of rough make and blunt terra-cotta features. He shouldered into an opening and struck his coin against the varnished pine. A barkeeper stopped and placed both hands on the bar.

"I'm hot, thirsty and broke," Donovan said with desperate cheerfulness. "Give me a shot of the worst whiskey in the place, and faith knows the best is bad enough."

The barman was glancing about for Tom Braga. Cary moved inside, seeing Braga come from the rear. When he swung past a table, Cary saw the bungstarter in his hip pocket. He was a grossly-fat man with a body shaped like a sack of potatoes. Cary had no use for him. His anxiety to be catering to other men's appetites glistened on him like sweat.

Donovan heard Braga approaching and turned to meet him. He did something which showed Sam Cary how desperate he was. He offered his hand to Braga. He said, "No hard feelings?"

Braga's hands rested on his hips. "No," he said. "But no whiskey, either." He smiled.

Donovan turned resignedly to the barkeeper. "A beer, then."

He slowly turned back as Braga said levelly, "And no beer."

Cary said from the door, "Is this any way to treat an old customer, Braga? Who's drunk more of your rotgut than Donovan? And it's pretty bum rotgut."

Braga's head turned. "Rotgut! My whiskey is bonded—" He observed Cary's smile and amended, "Anyway, it is good, for Cheyenne. Good enough for swilling."

"Then you can handle the by-products of swilling, such as ruined dispositions."

Donovan's voice was a growl. "Will you let me handle my own affairs, Cary? I'm buying for myself, right?"

"Wrong," Braga said.

Donovan's hand massaged the half-dollar. "I'm not a regular drunkard, man! I thought I was going out today and it would be my last drunk. But Mister Cary has decided to let us rot in Cheyenne a while longer. And the gods know I'm wanting a drink!"

Braga's glistening eyes savored the situation. "That's fine. Do your drinking at The Copperopolis, then. Or have they had enough of you, too?"

Donovan made a gesture of wiping his jaws with his palm. "No liquor, hey?"

"Not a drop. Get out."

"Damn you!"

Donovan roared it. "You'd let a man shake the hand of a pig like you and then deny him a drink!" The back of his hand smashed across Braga's mouth, rocking his head. He turned, took hold of a beer-cask in its cradle on the bar, and swung it about. Cutting the spigot open, he sank to his knees and let the foaming column spill into his mouth. Braga lunged back, the bungstarter in his hand. He swung at Donovan's head, and Donovan raised an arm and half-warded the blow. It landed with force enough to drop him to the floor.

Cary moved in quickly. They came from four points, the dishtoweled barmen armed with lengths of pool-cue. It was neatly planned, smoothly executed, and the only unplanned factors appeared to be Cary and John Silvertooth.

"Braga!" Cary shouted.

Leaning over the whacker with the mallet raised, Braga halted. He discovered the stein Cary had thrown at him. He ducked. It smashed into his shoulder, drenching him with beer.

Cary lunged into him, his eyes on Braga's pulpy

mouth. His fist collided with it with the good smack of a hand laid on a quarter of beef. Braga reeled into a table.

Cary heard a saloonman slide in behind him. A lamp cast the shadow of an arm. A houseman, short and deep-chested and with a red, congested face, chopped savagely at Cary's head with a truncated pool-cue. Cary fell away, raising his shoulder defensively. The club struck painfully against the bunched muscle. Cary set his teeth and lunged into the man. He caught the thick, corded throat with his hands, jammed him against the tall bar and hacked at the turgid face with the edge of his knuckles. The saloonman shouted and tried to writhe away. Cary gathered the power of his back and shoulder muscles in an overhand blow which smashed into the side of the man's jaw and turned it. He let the white face slide away.

The saloon crowd had shaped into a random crescent with Donovan, Cary and Silvertooth in the center and three of Braga's men carefully working in with pool-cue clubs at the ready. Cary looked at the ring of faces behind this shock-troop, thinking of loafer wolves. A tall man with a sallow, hairless face slanted in to chop at Donovan's head. Donovan caught the club in his hand, ripped it away and smashed the man across the nose. The houseman went to his knees, covering his face with his hands. Donovan bent, seized him by an arm and a leg and lifted him over his head. He crouched and straightened, hurling the man across the counter and into the stacked bottles of the back-bar.

He took time to seize Cary by the arm, then, his face dark with anger. "Get out of it!" he said. "I can handle six of their likes alone!"

"Can you handle one with a scattergun?" Silvertooth panted.

Donovan's bloodshot eyes comprehended slowly. He looked around for Tom Braga, but the saloonkeeper had disappeared. Donovan stood slope-shouldered and puzzled.

Now Cary heard a man and saw him fall back in the crowd and turn to thrust to the rear. It was like a signal, splitting the crowd and folding it back to front and rear; men were shouting their terror, and one raised an arm toward Cary as if to ward off a blow. Cary suddenly brought his fist down at the root of Donovan's neck, carrying him to the floor with him. He saw Braga's men fall back, getting out of line. It placed Tom Braga directly behind him, behind the bar, moving in with his double-barreled shotgun.

Cary crouched there, his hand grasping at the sawdust. Donovan was shouting curses and reaching for the edge of the bar. Cary rose suddenly and Braga was before him, a squat and greasy-faced man with a side-hammer shotgun prodding forward. Cary slapped his left hand down on the gun-barrel. His right hand flung sawdust into the saloonman's face.

He felt the shattering roar of the gun through his hand and arm. The charge flashed between him and Donovan. Overhead, the candles puffed out. Lamps burned at front and rear, and in the gloom men were lying on their bellies and clutching at the floor. Braga wrenched at the gun, his face distorted. Cary's hand slapped down on the hammers. He brought the gun-barrel up and around and Braga's grip was broken. Cary emptied the other charge into the ceiling. As he threw the gun aside, he saw Donovan vault the bar and trap Tom Braga against the back-bar. He saw his fist come back and drive in; cock and drive again, his head held slightly on the side. He watched Donovan release him. Braga turned and took one blind step toward the end of the bar, and collapsed.

Donovan turned back. The saloon was quiet. Donovan moved along the bar to the front, took a final look at the saloon and moved into the street. Cary and his wagonmaster lingered a moment and followed him.

Donovan was waiting on the walk. He said, "I suppose I should thank you, Mr. Cary?"

"I'd thank God, if I were you," Cary said. "Did you get your fill of beer?"

"I got more than that. I got a fist into the middle of a face I've been aching to spoil. But it's too bad it had to end the way it did."

"How's that?"

"With me beholden to you."

Smiling, Cary watched Donovan shoulder into the crowd gathering before the saloon.

Silvertooth had a puffiness under his eye and his calico shirt was ripped. Sourly, he observed Donovan's departure. "I could do with a whiskey, unless you're afraid I'd be throwing pig's-knuckles at somebody's nude."

"You'd be more likely," Cary said, "to be throwing looks at her."

2

Boothill Patrol

THE DAY FINISHED OUT IN A RED AND GRITTY DUSK.
Cary waited for dark before leaving for the rifle cache.
Supper fires puddled the dusk of the corral. A teamster
was frying venison in a long-handled iron skillet. From
south of town, the day-guard rode in from herding
stock.

It was all rough and casual, all utterly masculine.
Cary remembered how Gaybird Phillips used to drink
the strong liquor of whackers' yarns. How would it all
seem to her now, a grown woman, after two years away
from unshaven jowls, lumbering wagons, and dust—
fine dust, coarse dust; red dust and black dust?

He regarded her dearborn wagon, standing spruce-
topped among the burly freight wagons on the south
line. A thought came to him. Presently he walked to
his own wagon and struck a match. He grubbed in the
catchall box at the rear of it. He found something, and
slipped it into his pocket with the map. Moving si-

lently, he mounted the ladder at the back of the dearborn.

As he stepped through the flap, he heard a quick in-
take of breath. Cary's hand dropped to the warm
smoothness of brass and walnut at his thigh. In the
gloom, John Silvertooth spoke quickly.

"Now behave! I was just checking around."

Cary lighted the lamp. The light sparkled on a pair
of beaded gauntlets in the wagonmaster's hand. "I see."

In an excess of casualness, Silvertooth tossed them
on the cot. "First of these I ever seen that anybody but
a muleskinner could wear. Thought she'd like them."

Cary took a pair of moccasins from his pocket and
laid them on the bed. "I thought the same when I saw
these Blackfoot moccasins. She always did favor them.
I was wondering if that squaw got her sheets clean."

He pulled back the red-and-gray Indian blanket and
inspected the stiff cotton sheets.

"What's the difference?" Silvertooth grunted. "She
ain't going up with us."

"But she'll have a day or two in town."

They moved about hunting dust and insects. The
wagon contained a small chest, a commode, a goosefeather cot, a chair and a mirror. Cary moved to the
flap, and the wagonmaster said quickly, "She comes
tomorrow, eh?"

"You know that."

"I thought you maybe had something to tell me."

"Why should I have?"

Silvertooth said, "All right, I'll tell you something.
The first summer she came out after you put her in the
seminary, she told my missus something. She was fifteen, warn't she? She said you and her was married.
She said to keep it secret."

Cary's lips parted. He set them firmly together and
his hand rubbed his thigh. "She did, eh?"

"She did."

"How many washwomen has your wife told that to?"

"You know the answer to that. What I want to know is, what are you going to do about her?"

Cary found his pipe and packed it; he put it unlighted into his mouth. "Well, just so you won't think it's worse than it is. . . . You see, I never figured we were married. Old Bob Phillips made me promise to adopt her if anything happened to him. After the Uncpapas did for him, I took her to Cincinnati. But it seems bachelors weren't adopting fourteen-year-old girls that year. I tried to set her up in the seminary. But they reckoned that would make a kept woman out of her. So all I could do was marry her. Then I enrolled her in the school as Mrs. Samuel Cary."

"That's about how I laid it out," the wagonmaster said. "Still, that was then. What about now?"

Cary lighted the pipe. "I've heard Eastern women wear bleaching towels over their faces to keep their skin white. Gaybird will be a real Eastern lady. She'll take one look at the grease stains on my shirt and lose color. It will be an annulment or a divorce. . . ."

From the distant Laramie Hills, night sprawled across the prairie. They rode into the stiff rabbit brush, walking their mounts until they were clear of Stockwell's camp, a hundred yards west, and then letting them reach.

They put ten miles behind them; miles as devoid of individuality as the ties of the tracks they followed. But as they rode they looked about often, holding their ponies in to listen. Farther north, anywhere beyond the Platte, a night ride would be suicide. Down here there was chiefly the possibility of encountering a band of Ogallala Sioux out cutting telegraph wires.

A kangaroo rat bounded from the path of Cary's pony with a frightened chirp. The horse swerved; Cary hauled it around with an oath. He found he had flung his carbine up automatically.

Northwest he made out the flat bulk of a range of

hills. The landmark placed them a mile or so east of Sweetwater Coulee. According to Orrum's map, the wagon ought to be about two miles south of the tracks, hidden in the coulee.

Silvertooth glanced at him. "Am I gettin' womanly," he asked, "or do I smell Sioux?"

"You're gettin' womanly," Cary's horse shook bridle with a jingle of coin silver. The wind was redolent of sage. They dipped into a wallow and mounted again the dead level of the plain.

Cary grunted. "Hope the fool left the oxen on a stout picket."

Silvertooth's arm went up. "Yonder they are!"

"Crafty like a fool-quail!" Sam snorted. "Hide the wagons and leave the oxen in sight! Hell, there's three span of them. . . ."

They made it to be about two hundred feet to the gully on the bank of which stood the animals. Cary was on the point of touching his horse with his heels when suddenly his right arm extended to touch Silvertooth.

Silvertooth sat steadily in the saddle, staring. They saw one of the animals on the coulee's edge raise its head for an instant, scent and quietly go back to pulling tufts of grass. It was light enough to determine that they were not oxen. Nor did they carry saddles. They were Indian ponies.

They turned silently and retreated. Dismounting, Cary thumbed back the heavy spur of the bronze-framed Henry. Big John Silvertooth moored his calico mule to a clump of black sage. He removed his hat and dropped it on the ground. A bare head was his fighting trim.

Cary stared at the Indian ponies in the far darkness. The wind carried the faint stir of hoofs and a sound of voices. "Damn the army!" he muttered. "Those rifles could easily have been set down in Cheyenne."

Except for the army, they would not have been under a responsibility to take on a patrol of buck Indians to recover a wagonload of destruction. Their responsibil-

ity was to themselves and every other man who lived
north of Cheyenne. The tribe that got hold of a hundred
breech-loading Springfield rifles could clean out every
ranch and trading post on the Bozeman.

He stood close to Silvertooth. "Give me twenty minutes. I'll coyote around behind them. Try to belly up
to where you can see them."

"If they've tapped the whiskey," said the wagonmaster, "we can save our shells and tromp them out.
Shoot, maybe they ain't figured out how them guns
work, anyhow."

Cary walked north a quarter-mile to the tracks. He
cut west to the coulee and crossed on the trestle. Standing there, he searched the coulee but found no pickets.
He moved on. A nighthawk swooped low with a stiff
rush of feathers. On a far ridge, a coyote yelped. He
turned his head to seek the outlines of the ponies. Finding them, he went on more cautiously, leaving the trestle and pacing carefully through the brush.

He was within a hundred feet of the ponies when he
saw the Indian sitting cross-legged on the ground holding the reins. He sank down in a reaction of shock.

A full minute slid away. Cary knew that he was as
visible to the Indian as the Indian was to him, but the
sentry was watching what went on in the deep brush-
choked coulee. He was a young brave with a prairie
cock tail on his head. A dogskin quiver rode his shoulders. Cary read these signs and the clue of the pale
bullhide hanging on the horses, and they told him:
Sioux. A little gang of green Ogallala warriors out
hunting lonely stage tenders to murder or supernatural
buffalo to kill, feats to make men of them in the lodges.

As he rose, he winced at the leathery creaking of his
boots. He made out a sound of stone on wood, a deep-
throated voice raised briefly in a laugh. The warrior
rocked forward to look into the wash.

Sam raised his arm high in a signal. He breathed
deeply, flexing his arms to ease the tautness out of them.

He held the carbine lightly and began moving up behind the horses.

Now he could glimpse the action in the coulee through the tumble of boulders and brush on the stony slope. A tiny fire burned against the sand. Five Indians in hip-length leather shirts, breech-clouts and leggings were busy about a freight wagon. One stood in the wagon. Two others were attempting to yoke a span of oxen to the wagon. The rest were occupied in opening crates with rocks or in examining the guns. There was no sign or smell of whiskey. A young buck raised a rifle to his cheek and sighted it, the barrel lining precisely on Cary. His heart exploded in his breast. But an instant later the brave lowered the gun and shook it as if to hear it rattle.

Cary settled his feet in the gravel, his left shoulder to his target, his right elbow extended. His finger pains-takingly took up trigger slack. The gun barrel lifted with a roar, the butt thrusting solidly against the packed muscles of his shoulder. He pulled the loading lever and sprinted forward. He saw the seated Indian lurch forward and sprawl out into the coulee.

The tight huddle of ponies split open like a dropped melon. Two ponies plunged into the wash. A Sioux seized the mane of one and swung himself across its back. He turned and fired a carbine at Cary as his heels hammered the horse's ribs. The shot went through the brush with a rattle of broken twigs. The brave vanished in the dark.

A man was running along the bank with a thud of boots. A large and reassuring shadow, John Silvertooth sprawled at the lip of the barranca and lay in the brush with only his head exposed. His gun pointed like a finger at the Indian in the wagon, who was crouched in the deep bed with a gun thrust between the side-boards.

Sprawling opposite him, Cary heard the slam of the brave's gun. Grit exploded in his face, cutting his fore-head in a wide and dull pattern of pain. He fired back and saw the splintered hole where the ball went through the wagon-side. He could hear the brave moving in the wagon. Then the flash of Silvertooth's rifle illuminated the coulee and the Indian in the freight wagon moved convulsively.

Running low, an Ogallala jumped the wagon tongue, shot past the single yoke of oxen, and made for a break in the creekbed. Cary fired. As the pouring echoes faded, he saw the brave writhing on the sand.

Somewhere, out of sight below the rim of the bank, two more coppery bodies moved, heard but unseen. Cary waited, thinking more about the man who had ridden up the wash. He lay still, alert for the tread of moccasins behind him. Then he heard a soft rush below. A hand came into sight on the rim of the wash. The Indian got his hold and vaulted up six feet in front of him, wide-stanced and stooped, a stocky warrior in a red breech-clout and long shirt. He searched the darkness for an instant before discovering Cary. He held a short-axe stolen from the wagon. Suddenly finding the long shape asprawl before him, he hurled himself forward.

Cary fired and rolled away. The Indian struck the ground, pinning Cary's legs. He moved spasmodically. A moment later Cary became aware that the remaining warrior had lunged up the bank below John Silvertooth, a rifle raised in his hands like a war-club. Silvertooth fired once and the man turned and slid down the bank.

They lay there. There was a confused sound of oxen lunging about, chained to the wheels and unable to escape. Silvertooth's voice came "Sam?"

"All right. You?"

"Fit. Heard anything out of that other one?"

"I'm listening."

They waited twenty minutes before they descended to the wash. The Sioux were out of action, the guns unharmed, but Cary could not relax. "I'd give half the guns to have that one back. Did you see the shields on their ponies? Those were Thunder Fighters, Esconella's blood brothers. . . .''

Silvertooth halted in the act of searching out a keg of whiskey. He straightened. "Hell!" he said.

Cary unchained the oxen. "I'm not afraid of losing their love—but damn it! These breech-loaders were going to be a surprise."

"Maybe they hadn't figured them out."

A realistic man, Cary did not answer. Silvertooth came to help him handle the oxen, and presently Sam threw off the whole notion of Indians with a shake of his head. "If we don't get back before sunup and throw this one in line with the others, you can write off the rifles anyhow."

Bill Orrum came from the hot and windy night into The Nations. The trader moved with a loose, easy slouch. He wore a leather shirt, leather breeches and moccasins; his black pigtails were tied with greasy knots.

A crowd of railroad workers were hoorawing at the bar. Orrum found a table near a chuckaluck game. He bought a bottle of whiskey and poured his drink. He thought of Sam Cary. Orrum, the pigtailed, dark dweller of wilderness places, was not an overproud man, but he knew how to bring a resentment to maturity.

He thought about the trip up the Bozeman Trail to the Montana mines, which was to think about Indians. For thirty years he had taken care of himself in this country. He had got along because he was like his hosts—silent, savagely practical, vigilant; not too hankering toward luxuries. Yet for the sins of other white men he must pay, also, and the price was smokeless fires and sleeping away from his camp. If trouble came, he counted on his pay-load to get him through. He carried a hundred and fifty ancient smoothbore muskets the army had abandoned in a warehouse twenty years ago. These could be sold decently in Butte—or traded for his scalp.

Darkness came and he was aware of Mark Stockwell in the doorway. Seeing him, Stockwell approached and sat at the table where Orrum drank whiskey and played solitaire, a man very much alone.

"Cary and Silvertooth just left camp," the trader said shortly. He was perspiring. A man of massive strength, he had a firm and compact make; his chest was deep and his neck short. He looked to Orrum like a man it would be easier to kill than to hurt, insulated from injury by the slow and easy power of his body.

"Watching Cary middling close, ain't you?" Orrum remarked.

Stockwell's eyes were sourly displeased. "You didn't sell him the guns?"

Orrum poured again from the bottle. "He raised the money. I hadn't got any choice."

Stockwell pressed the heel of his fist against the table with slow and bitter force. "Damn it! I'd have given fifty dollars apiece for those rifles. Why didn't you come to me first?"

"I didn't go to him. Cary came to me, six months ago, as soon as the army said no guns. I tried to save them for you. When are you putting out?"

"Can't say. Before Cary, I hope. You'll go back to Independence?"

Orrum turned a green glass ring on his finger. "Montana."

Stockwell's thick brows raised. "Up the Bozeman?"

"How else?"

"What for? You're traded out, aren't you?"

Orrum's eyes had a spark of humor. "You're full of wonders about other people's business tonight."

Stockwell had a tenacious and unhumorous mind. He turned to signal a bartender and again stared into the shiny, tautskinned features. "You may as well travel with me. You'd better travel with some train."

"I figure I'm better off alone than with somebody the Sioux don't like."

"Such as me?"

"You and the younger set get along. The whiskey drinkers. The warrior societies. I've heard you and Esconella meet behind the barn and smoke the pipe together."

Temper stiffened Stockwell's lips. "Is that what you hear?"

"I hear it direct," said Orrum. "I wouldn't trust him too far, you know. Esconella may be a chief's son-in-law, and the old man may be paralyzed, but—I wouldn't trust any of them. The purtiest sight in the world is an Injun's back—in your rifle sights."

"I don't worry about the Sioux. I'm north of their grounds. But it pays to keep right with all of them. What are you taking along?"

"Trade goods."

"Beads and tobacco, eh—and a bunch of guns?"

"A few old cannons the army gave up long ago."

"Trade guns," Stockwell said.

"Why, Mark!" Orrum said. "Trade guns for Injuns?"

Stockwell grunted, seeming offended that the idea had been given words. "Don't be a damned fool. I live up there too, you know. I don't want guns in their hands any more than Cary."

"Of course the Sioux don't range about your post, though, if you wanted to get rid of some betwixt here and Cary's place. They've got gold these days, since they learned what it was for and Wells Fargo put it in their way."

Stockwell's first reaction was a slowness to grasp it. Then his brows pulled in and he said softly, "You've rubbed up against too many of them. You've taken their ways."

Orrum said, "This is their country, Mark. You take their ways if you want to get along. And you ain't going to get along whilst Cary's splitting the business with you.''

''I can get along without putting guns in their hands.''

''If Cary don't shut you out first. The army will be back. Maybe not this year; likely next. He's a sharp trader, Mark. When the travel is going up the Bozeman instead of shortcutting him by going around, why, you'll see what I mean. You had a year of bucking him before the army ducked out, didn't you? Kind of slim tradin', I'll reckon.''

A smoke of resentment fumed in Stockwell's eyes, as though he were angry at the trader for having brought something up which was better left unthought of. He finished his whiskey and stood up.

''I'll be leaving tomorrow night. Meet us up the line if you want to go along.''

''Thanks,'' Orrum said.

Cary awoke at sunup, when the bugles at Fort Russell began sounding their mixed glee of brassy calls. He heard his whackers turning out. Ironware clanged and burning mesquite roots sent their smoky incense about the corral. Lost sleep and reaction from the night's activity dulled him.

Quitting his blankets, which lay under a wagon, he stood in the harsh sunlight and pulled on his shirt. The arms-wagon occupied its place in the hollow square of freight-wagons. Neither the first nor the last, it was merely another great-wheeled Murphy with its tongue run up under the wagon ahead. They had terminated the drive from Sweetwater Coulee two hours before sunrise.

Cary somberly regarded the stork-like tank by the tracks, slowly dripping water into the salt-crusted puddle beneath it. He resented the trash about camp and the shirtless men yawning their way through pre-breakfast chores. This, thank God, was their last day in Cheyenne.

Today Gaybird Phillips came. There would be the difficulty of explaining to her why she must not make the trip to the border this summer. There would be the task of getting her back on a train tomorrow. And then everything would simplify, and he could slot his problems plainly enough—yoke the oxen and turn them north.

As he ate, he took notice of a buoyancy among the men. They were all as sick of the camp as he was. They looked forward to the trail, with all its dangers. Breakfast over, he gave the order to slip the wheels and tar every axle. Before the job was finished, the men were glancing up the tracks, anticipating the arrival of the passenger train. Work trains hammered through from the supply depot, heading west.

A little after noon, the telegrapher's key rattled in the small yellow station with its two mud chimneys. The station master came from the door to flap a sheet of paper.

"She comes! Forty-five minutes."

Cary killed some more time, his mind trying phrase after phrase. How to tell the girl without hurting her feelings? But better a hurt feeling than a lost scalp.

He started to move to the station to await the train, and then something caused him to glance at the loading dock across from the yellow railroad shack. In the bleached yellow sunlight, Donovan's barrels still stood awaiting removal. Silvertooth had come up beside him. Cary was conscious of his testy gaze as he, too, regarded the barrels. Cary removed his Stetson and sliced perspiration from his forehead with his finger, and then replaced the hat and said, "I reckon Donovan's forgotten those barrels."

They crossed the corral and stood by the rear of Donovan's lead-wagon. The two trailers were packed, but the gate of the main wagon was down and from the half-packed interior drifted a vapor of tobacco. Cary looked at the big man sprawling against a stanchion. Suddenly

discovering him, Donovan casually swung his legs
overside. He regarded Cary with a shallow mask of
respect. "You've got four barrels on the dock," Cary
said.

"Sure, no one told me," said Donovan blandly.

"Someone's told you now. Silvertooth will help you
move them. Unpack them all and repack the goods in
the wagon."

The Irishman tucked a thumb under his belt. "I've
heard it said Mark Stockwell is the best freighter in
Wyoming. He carries his goods in the barrels they come
in. Why can't you?"

"I'm not selling barrels. Why should I carry them?"

Donovan frowned, but after a moment, his hazel eyes
not leaving Cary's face, he began to smile craftily, and
from his pocket he brought a small handful of coins.
He glanced down at them. There was still the fifty-cent
piece Silvertooth had loaned him, but there were, in
addition, glints of gold. He looked beyond the men, at
others of the bullwhackers who were within earshot.
His expression subtly changed.

"Mr. Cary," he said, in bluff and artificial good-
nature, "you can do what you damned please with your
barrels. I'm quitting."

"You can't quit," Silvertooth snapped. "You're into
us for sixty dollars."

Donovan turned Cary's palm up and triumphantly
dropped six goldpieces upon it. "I got onto that a week
ago. You wouldn't shanghai a man, but you'd let him
drink himself into your debt before he found out what
kind of a circus he was into. I say this evens us up. I
talked with Mark Stockwell on the way back. He ad-
vanced me the money to pay you off. I'm going to Montana with him."

Cary tossed the coins in his hand in mild wonder. He
looked up at Donovan and saw him braced for trouble.
He chuckled and set the coins on the wagonbed.

"You're a quick-headed Mick. Only you can't buy out of my army, the way you did Uncle Sam's."

"Can't I?" said Donovan. "I reckoned I already had."

Cary's eyes ran over him, as they had that first day the Irishman came looking for work, hunting flaws and not finding any. His shoulders were sloping and massive, blotched with large freckles. The smell of him was of whiskey gone sour and sweat upon sweat. He was a testy and tough man, something for the wilderness to bruise its knuckles on. Donovan's eyes doggedly met his for a moment, and then slid down to a point on Cary's buckskin shirt and held there.

Cary asked quietly, "What's the matter, Donovan? Do we make the coffee too strong for you?"

"No," Donovan growled. "You set a man to do a boy's chore—repacking a wagon that's sound as a knot. We've been ready to move for five days. But we police and cook and stand guard until a man'd think he was back in the army. And we'll kape on doing it, until Mr. Cary's young lady comes on the train. You'd let ten tons of pork rot rather than miss the chance of hauling a hundred and ten pounds of young female to your post."

Cary heard the careful silence of the camp. A man casually walked between Donovan's wagon and the next, stopping where he could watch. A muscle rippled under the smooth mahogany of Cary's jaw.

"We can leave the young lady out of it," he said mildly. "Are you afraid of the Sioux. Or of me?"

Donovan's eyes lighted. He stood before the trader, a strapping man with a splayed nose and protruding ears. He stood taller than Cary and outweighed him. Cary saw in his eyes that he had been long at the brawler's evil of comparing. Donovan's thumb gouged at the bowl of his pipe. "I don't fear the Sioux," he said, "and I ain't yet met the man I fear."

"That's fine," Cary said. "It doesn't do to fear Indians: They smell it on you, like a dog. And I like a man that will stand up to another. That's why I'm glad you're coming with us.''

Donovan looked puzzled. ''I told you I was going with Stockwell. I had the advance so's I could pay you off.''

''Did Stockwell know how you were going to use it?''

''It's my say how I use it.''

''Not when you use it to put a man in a hole. No trader worth a damn would lend you money to leave another short a hand. Nobody but a trader like Stockwell. You'll take it back to him.''

Donovan grinned maliciously. ''You weren't afraid of leaving the army in a hole when you loaned me the money to buy out, were you?''

Cary's eyes puckered thoughtfully. ''Maybe they knew what they were doing, at that. Maybe they'd already tagged you, the way they do a blown-out musket. *I. & C.*, eh? Inspected and Condemned. . . .''

Donovan's weight leaned forward onto his toes. He put his hand up to tap Cary's chest; but it hung there and he pointed a scarred forefinger. ''I done two hitches, Cary! I seen Fetterman throw his command away to Red Cloud, and after that anything in brass made me sick. The army never condemned me: I condemned them.''

''Then you should like my army. Not an officer in the lot.'' His hand curled the brim of his hat. ''Get onto the barrels as soon as you've returned Stockwell's money.''

Donovan's boots stirred and his shoulders made a settling shrug. Cary looked into his corded red face without emotion, until Donovan's eyes moved away again, and he said, ''A man might as well be in the infantry.'' He picked up the money, tossed it once in his hand, and sauntered off through the wagons.

''A rebel!'' Silvertooth snorted. ''A copper-bottomed rebel! There'll be trouble with him, I tell you.''

Cary breathed deeply. "He won't make trouble. He's just letting me know that he leads better than he pushes."

Silvertooth strolled to the barrels to await the bull-whacker's return. Cary walked up the tracks, stepped onto the splintered station platform and sat on a bench, one leg extended, the other cocked across it, letting his muscles take their ease.

He looped up as a short, toughly-made man in buck-skin pants and a spotted calico shirt crossed the tracks and vaulted carelessly onto the platform, recognizing Cary with a lazy hand salute. The man took a place on the bench, sopping perspiration from his forehead with a handkerchief.

"I wisht some Sioux outfit," he said, "would whoop up a rain dance and break this weather."

"Any time the Sioux break the weather for us," said Cary, "it will rain arrows."

He kept his eyes and his good-nature from Coy Mullan. Mullan was Mark Stockwell's wagonmaster, and that was enough. He was also a transplanted Texan who wore one pant-leg in his boot and one out, and that was too much. He affected a knife in his right boot and wore a Dragoon pistol deep on his right thigh.

Mullan lighted a cigar. "I hear we've got important company coming on the train. Envoy from the Great White Father to Crazy Dog. Man named Merritt."

"God help us, then!" Cary said. "We'd almost lived down the trouble the last envoy made."

"It's time for a peace talk. The Piegans raided down into the Gallatin Valley last month, before we left. If they team up with the Sioux, we're both finished."

"I thought Stockwell kept them all happy with stick candy and Forty-Rod whiskey?"

Mullan smiled. "He could show you some tricks, at that. He smokes the peace pipe with them with one hand and steals their buffalo robes for a dime apiece with the other."

"He'll get his scalp tanned in the bargain, one of these days."

Mullan chuckled, a calm and hard-featured man not easily roused. He was a sort of middleman in the distaste of these traders one for another. He grinned around his cigar. "What's the real trouble between you and Mark? You don't neither of you talk much."

"Some people claim that's a virtue."

Mullan took this impassively. He let his eyes drift off toward the wagon camp. "What's different about your outfit today?" he frowned.

Cary's eyes touched him quickly. Then he shrugged. "Maybe the trash has been picked up."

". . . Twenty-four wagons last night, twenty-five today. Breeding them?"

"I picked up a wagon from an emigrant outfit last night," Cary said. "They'd quit it. Oxen broke down and I bought it for the cost of the goods."

"Washtubs and churns and wimmen's fixings?" Mullan inquired.

Cary's eyes went to his face. "What are you getting at?"

"Do I have to be getting at something?" Mullan winked. "I was going to say that if you wanted to park any of your wagons in our camp today, Stockwell says it would be okay. We've already stood inspection. There's a sergeant named Casner that can smell powder and ball through six layers of duck."

"Am I carrying powder and ball?"

Mullan rose unhurriedly, pulled on the cigar and removed it to regard the smoldering tip. "You're cagey today, Sam. But Mark and I figure we've got to lend each other a hand in this trade, if we're going to get by at all."

"Help me by keeping out of my way, then. How much was he going to charge me for this helping hand? Half the arms he thinks I'm carrying?"

Mullan looked at him and kept most of his anger out

of his flat, ruddy features. "You figure you don't have much to learn about freighting, eh?"

Cary saw the raw end of Mullan's patience, and pleasantly pinked it again. "One of the first things I learned was never to trust a man who wore one britches-leg in and one out."

"You go to hell!" Mullan snapped.

Cary began to chuckle. "I forgot about you Texans, Coy. Proud and sensitive as a fat Comanch' full of corn beer."

Mullan's eye flicked and his hands formed slowly into fists. Then he said brusquely, "Good luck with the army. I hope I'm around when you take 'em on."

Cary's laughter followed him across the tracks.

Afterward Cary's face sobered. It was plain enough that Stockwell knew of the gun transaction with Bill Orrum. He was in a position to sic the army on Cary, and if he did not, it would not be ethics which re-strained him. Cary was not sure what the commandant at Fort Russell would do if he had the report of the rifles. He was not sure what he would do himself.

Then he heard a man bawl three words: *"Yonder she comes!"*

3

Bad Trouble — In Calico

DOWN THE STRING-STRAIGHT FILAMENTS OF STEEL Cary discerned a smudge of smoke. He heard his bull-whackers running up the platform and he felt the sting of Silvertooth's palm on his back. Silvertooth said as he passed, "She's eighteen now, Sam! Hard candy and pacifiers won't work no more on the lady."

The train acquired color and form and sound—a chunky little diamond-stack drawing six cars, breathing dust and smoke, alkali crusting the dented boiler jacket and brass steam dome. The locomotive coasted past the station and halted, exuding heat and rusty water, a snowy feather of steam dissolving into the deep blue of the sky. From its black iron bowels escaped strange digestive noises. Trainmen dropped to the ground and a wagonload of cordwood whipped up to the tender. Passengers began to appear slowly. A conductor in a linen duster, his face bloated with heat, swung from the observation car. Mail bags were tossed to the ground.

Suddenly, down the line of coaches sitting unevenly on the tracks, through the crowd and an abrupt cloud of dirty steam, Sam saw her. Behind a bulwark of three black India-rubber bags stood a winsome figure in a bottle-green gown and a white basque, a frilled parasol over her shoulder. She waved at him, but he still stood there, astonished. What had happened to her, the girl in pigtails? She was gone, and in her place stood a young woman he had never seen before. Cary went forward.

He took her hands as he reached her, smiling as she laughed up at him. "Sam, it's so wonderful!"

He felt the small fingers through the starched mesh gloves. "So a stage isn't good enough for you any more!"

She wrinkled her nose at the train, floury with alkali. "Those things! Shake you to pieces!"

"What's a dearborn do?"

"Rocks me to sleep," she declared. ". . . Sam, about here you used to kiss me."

"Godfather's privilege?" He bent and kissed her cheek. She was a small and animated presence, bell-shaped with her full skirts and snugly-fitted summer basque. He straightened, half-ashamed of himself; but he found the girl in pigtails slipping away from him, taking with her his own attitude toward her. His tendency was to regard her as someone new and desirable.

Gaybird's hair was as black as ever, lustrous with brushing. In the way the gray eyes, black-lashed, looked at him there was something more personal—as though they were focused on him instead of the whole, bright world.

He turned and weighed the bags. "Traveling heavier. You can thin it out tonight, unless you want me to put a couple of bulls in the traces. I took a room for you at the Rollins House."

Gaybird inspected him curiously as they moved along the platform. "Didn't you bring my wagon?"

"Sure. But the camp's pretty rough."

"I was brought up to consider hotels an affectation. We'll cancel the room." Then she caught his arm. Before the station stood an attractive red-haired girl with a dour-looking man of middle age who wore a talma cape over his shoulders. "See her?"

The girl was looking at them. He saw her smile, and a moment later the red-haired girl called, "Don't forget! You're to look us up."

"The Rollins House? I won't," Gaybird promised.

Cary met the girl's eyes for a moment. They were sage-green, and not shy. Neither were they bold, but with a quality of challenge in them. The man in the talma did not acknowledge them. He was absorbing the hot and dusty panorama with a stricken look. "He's a government man," Gaybird said. "An envoy to the Indian Nations. She's pretty, isn't she?"

Cary considered. "Not to say provocative. Is the name Merritt?"

"How did you know?"

"I heard he was a coming. I hope he likes it up there in the Bighorns. He doesn't look like the type who would."

They met Silvertooth. He had a hug and a kiss for her. "Hard trip, lassie?"

"Those trains!"

Silvertooth chuckled and looked the girl over. "Will she toughen up to it again, do you think?" he asked Sam.

"She hasn't decided for sure that she's going. Either way, we leave at sunup. Let the men go. Give Donovan five dollars, but don't let him out of your sight."

As they crossed the tracks, Gaybird stared archly up at him. Cary's shoulders were nervously taut under the leather shirt, but his randomly-sketched face did not give him away: All his practice skirmishing was nullified by the total femininity of this girl.

They passed a coal yard. "So I haven't decided whether I'm going?" Gaybird remarked.

"Gay, we've got to talk about it."

A change came to her face, a thoughtfulness that firmed her lips. ". . . All right, Sam."

They made a perilous crossing of the street through freight outfits grinding by with the hard language of whackers and the sour stench of buffalo robes. A man in a derby and striped jersey was wrestling beer barrels from a dray. He stopped to look at her; Cary was obliquely flattered: She was a dainty and memorable spectacle for Cheyenne.

They reached the hotel. He had a wish deeper than a sigh: That they might have been meeting for the first time today—that for them it did not go back to a time when she was thirteen and he was her father's partner.

Spurs jangled on the sheet-metal floor of the dining room. At red-and-white ginghamed tables, train passengers were gulping down their food, alert for the train bell. Gaybird made herself comfortable before giving him her attention. She disposed of the parasol and then, linking her fingers, looked soberly at him until she laughed.

"Sam, you're so funny!"

"What do you mean—funny?"

"So stern. What's the matter? Are you wondering how to make me drink my milk?" Cary scratched his neck. She watched him in amusement. "And what's this about my not going up to the fort?" she demanded.

"It's the same trouble as last summer, only worse. I wrote you that the army had pulled out. I saw the ashes of Fort Phil Kearney a week after the troopers rode out. How many emigrants and miners do you think are going up the Bozeman this year, without even the protection of a few hundred green recruits?"

She tried to be serious. "Why, I don't know, Sam. How many?"

He tapped the table. "An outfit went out last week.

Those were the first wagons this summer. They may be the last. There's a reason. The Bozeman road may be two hundred miles closer than any other route, but no road is a shortcut when you die on the way.''

"But we've always been friendly with the Ogallalas, haven't we?"

"With Crazy Dog's Ogallalas. He's got a crazy son-in-law named Esconella, now, who's spoiling for fight. And Crazy Dog's sick—sick in the legs. How big a chief is a paralyzed chief? If Esconella can tie enough yellow scalps to his lance when he goes out to proselyte warriors, then Crazy Dog is out of it. And we've got a war on our hands.''

With devious feminine logic, Gaybird pointed out, "But he can't take scalps if the trail isn't being used, can he?''

Sam smiled. "No, and we can't make money. But he'd have nothing against bullwhackers' scalps, and there's a couple of trains I know of going out tomorrow.''

Her chin lifted. "You're not frightening me, Sam Cary. We built the fort when the Indians were unfriendly, and we can certainly hold it against them now.''

"Suppose they besiege? Fifteen hundred braves piling logs against the walls could cause a lot of damage.''

He saw the hurt in her eyes, and he laid his hand over hers.

"I'm sorry, Gay. It's not much of a welcome-home, is it? This kind of talk never built anything. But that's the situation, and I'd be second cousin to a murderer to take a woman into it. That's why I said what I did to Silvertooth. And that's why I say I want you to take the train back to Cincinnati tomorrow.''

Gaybird's hand was at her throat. She pulled a thin gold chain from the bosom of her dress and showed him the wedding band laced onto it. Her face was very young and very pretty and very solemn.

"I don't want to embarrass you, Sam, but—do you want this back? Is that what you're trying to say?"

Sam had not seen the ring since that day four years ago. He turned it briefly in his fingers. He saw that it had been engraved inside.

Sam and Gaybird, August 12, 1864

He looked quickly at her, but she pulled the ring away and dropped it back into her bosom. "I was a sentimental child, wasn't I? I did that after you left."

"I suppose we've got to do something about it," Cary sighed. "It's going to be awkward if somebody comes to ask me for your hand, and I have to tell them you happen to be my wife!"

She laughed, but the moment was stiff.

"I think we ought to remember what your father wanted for you," Sam said. "He wanted to make his stake out here and go back East. He didn't want you to have to pick a man from a couple of dozen bullwhackers and buffalo hunters. He used to talk about the streets in his home town. Shade trees, and painted houses, and galleries like the decks of a steamboat."

Her gray eyes watched his lips while he spoke. "How do you know I want those things? I've just come from white houses and shade trees. I'm dying for mountain meadows and snow creeks. They're *my* idea of home."

Cary frowned. "I'm the wrong man to tout the East and run down the West. But let's not forget Esconella and his Thunder Fighters. And the Sand Creek Desert."

"You forget those things when the danger is over," Gaybird stated. "But you remember the mountains."

A waiter came. He took their order and departed. They did not meet each other's eyes. Something simple, thought Cary, had been made into something complex by a mumbling parson. She was essentially someone he had never met before. Yet a backlog of memories kept him from treating her like a charming stranger.

Suddenly she asked, "Sam—do you think marriages are made in heaven?"

"I think this particular marriage was made in a preacher's parlor," he smiled wryly. "I remember you were so tired from the train that you almost went to sleep during the ceremony. If God entered this one in the book, he must have entered it in pencil so it could be rubbed out."

"But it was still a marriage. And we can't just ignore it. That would be sinful."

"Sin," Cary conjectured, "is for preachers." He said pointedly, "If any notion of responsibility to a certain bullwhacker who needs a haircut and a clean shirt is on your mind, forget about it."

She raised her brows. "Oh, but I don't feel obligated! Only, I think we ought to decide what we're going to do."

What needed to be done was perfectly clear, thought Cary. Yet he could not make himself use the word. He found himself hedging from his bound duty.

He said, "The first thing is to settle the fort business. I'm prepared to buy you out. I wish I could give all cash, but I can't. I thought of a price of fifteen thousand for your share. I'll give you—"

Her eyes fascinated him. They were gray as a winter sky, but in no way cold. They were bright and noticing and alive. They watched him hesitate over the figures.

"One thing we can agree on right now," she declared. "Indians or no Indians, I'm going back to Fort Graybull. It happens to be my home. If I'm selling my home, I want to see it again first, if only to appraise it. That's reasonable, isn't it?"

Cary leaned back, his eyes unaccountably warm. "It would seem reasonable to a woman, I expect."

Gaybird gasped in astonishment. "Why, Sam! That

makes it practically an anniversary after all! It's the first time you've ever admitted I was a grown-up woman!''

In the dearborn, closely warm, and smelling of dust and creosote, Gaybird removed her basque and vest, unpinned the glistening dark *couronne* of her hair and stood before the mirror. Gaybird Cary—Gaybird Phillips, that was—had never looked so before this mirror, she thought. She felt like a young matron visiting a niece's room. Everywhere were the tokens of girlhood, small treasures of her life in Wyoming. They seemed in surprisingly bad taste, some of them; all of them marvelously young.

Released, her hair hung in two braids coming across her shoulders. Her bosom was small but not too small. Soon her skin would darken with the stain of weather. Her eyes would appear lighter. Her lower lip was deep and rich.

Remembered impressions touched her, fragrant camp suppers in the heart of the squared wagons. A French harp singing in the prairie darkness; ungainly teamsters being awkwardly attentive. She was glad to be back.

She could hear Sam kicking up a fire and Silvertooth setting a dutch oven and coffee pot on it. Their voices were low, but she remained quiet, and presently they forgot to be careful and she could hear them.

''Takes up where she left off, don't she?'' That was Silvertooth.

''About Sand Creek, Cincinnati may begin to remember pretty fine,'' Sam contended.

''You couldn't talk her out of going with us?''

''She's set on it.''

''Well—this country needs women, of course,'' said Silvertooth.

''You talk like a breeder,'' Cary told him.

''Who takes better care of his stock than a breeder? We need women, and she's got her old man's toughness. No, I reckon you don't see it. You see 'seminary' all over her. But you'll see what I mean. Heat and sand won't change her none. If she's for Wyoming, you've got a pardner for keeps.''

Silvertooth yawned, then. ''I'll git uptown and keep an eye on the boys. A reg'lar brawl would set us back another forty-eight hours. *'Noches.*'' His boots moved off.

Gaybird smiled, poured water in a basin and washed. Then she dressed again, left the wagon and joined Sam for the rude camp meal.

She was washing the dishes when they heard boots stepping casually through the darkness toward them. It was Mark Stockwell. Hatless, Stockwell's crisp hair was ruddy in the light. He made Gaybird a nod and faced Cary after a moment's idle scrutiny of the camp.

''Camp looks trim. Putting out tomorrow?''

''Maybeso. You?''

Stockwell smiled. ''Maybeso. I was just talking to Major Drew, at the fort, about you.''

Cary stared at him. ''You know we're in this together, don't you? If I get inspected, I'll see to it that every last scrap of gear you're carrying is set down.''

The trader raised a glowing branch to start a cigar. ''This wasn't about freight. It was about taking some passengers. This man, Merritt—the envoy—needs escort to the Bighorns. It seems Drew can't give escort, because the trail is off-limits. He wanted my advice and I suggested you, your place being close to Crazy Dog's grounds.''

''That's fine. Only I don't guide. Not for the army.''

''Then here's your chance to get right with the army.''

Cary picked up his coffee cup and swirled it. ''What's this fellow expected to do? Arrange a treaty single-handed?''

''He's a sort of flunky to lay down the rug for the real treaty parley. He'll feel out the Ogallalas. If they're amenable, he'll arrange for a full-scale parley at Fort

Laramie this fall—feathers and brass and medals, all the usual la-de-da.''

''What's he like?''

''Cold as yesterday's dishwater. His wife's a beauty. Too bad she isn't the envoy. She could pacify me, I'll bet. They're waiting in the major's office right now. I said I'd send you up.''

Cary finished the coffee. ''They'll have a wait, then, I can't leave Gaybird alone.''

''That's the part of this mission I like best,'' Stockwell smiled. ''I'll take charge of Miss Phillips until you come back. I'd like her opinion of some dress goods I'm taking up, anyway. If she likes it, there's a bolt for her.''

Annoyance shaded Cary's face, but Gay spoke quickly. ''Sam, you must! Could anyone guide him better than you?''

Cary sighed and pulled his hat from the bag where it rested. ''Nobody could guide him more reluctantly. All that will come of it is slow travel, and sunburn for Merritt. The army will nullify whatever he accomplishes. But I'll talk to them.''

In the silent blackness before dawn, the Fort Graybull outfit broke camp. With a grind of tires rocking across the railroad tracks, the wagons pulled into the long column. The sounds were heavy and muffled, of oxen lunging along with gaunt heads swinging, of spokes and axles mumbling to themselves in the roil of white night dust. A few miles ahead moved the gray ghost of Mark Stockwell's train: Stockwell had broken camp just far enough ahead of Cary to get the lead, with its advantages of clean waterholes and fresh graze.

At Fort Russell, Cary rode inside to pick up the Army ambulance which would carry the Indian envoy and his wife. The commandant, and Cary's own good sense, had prevailed over his prejudice: Better to work with the army than against it. He would provide escort to Doctor Merritt.

In a week, Cary made Fort Laramie and quitted it. North of Cheyenne, Laramie was sanctuary. Beyond Laramie, security was a man's own problem. The nearest walls, beyond burned ones, were at Fort Graybull, on the border, two hundred miles away.

Moving deeper into Indian country, a primitive sort of despatch governed each action; and back of this tautness of order marched the shadow which was its cause.

Short of ruined Fort Reno, on the Dry Fork of Powder River, Cary caught sight of the Montana wagons on a ridge a few miles ahead. During the noon layover, Stockwell came loping back with Coy Mullen. He pulled in beside Cary to hand him a shard of pottery.

Cary frowned and turned it over. "Where'd you find it?"

"Inside the fort. There's the rubbish of a big camp."

"How many bucks?"

"I make it a hundred and fifty," Mullan said.

Cary tossed the pottery aside. "What do you want to do about it?"

"Team up. We've got to—for security. Fifty wagons are better medicine than twenty-five."

Cary shrugged. "I'd rather know where my enemies are than have to guess at it."

The muscles of Stockwell's jaws creased. "Have your joke. But you've got women to think of. I'll hold off squaring-up tonight until you let me know."

Cary did have women to think of: He knew that, and it was the only thing which could have made him travel double with Mark Stockwell. He said, "All right—for the women. But we'll travel wagon and wagon, and the security plan will be mine."

Stockwell nodded briefly. He rode back to his train.

Breaking out of the layover, Cary helped Doctor Merritt hitch his mules. Then he mounted his own pony and held it by the forewheels of the ambulance.

"Easier traveling from here on," he smiled. "We hit Fort Reno tonight. We'll join up with Stockwell, for less dust and more security. Then we head up into God's country—where there's water for shaving again."

"I'll believe there's water when I see it," Merritt replied grimly.

"And when we see it," Dale Merritt, his wife, smiled, "we won't recognize it for mud."

"You'll recognize this," Cary promised.

Merritt tooled the team along through the rising dust. "Some time you might give me a tip on how to get around these head-hunters I'm to parley with. They say there's a way to make a fool of any man."

"I wouldn't recommend making a fool of these people," Cary said. "Not of Crazy Dog. He may be old and half-crippled, but he's still the big chief. He's got a son-in-law, Esconella, who'd like to depose him, but you'll still deal with Crazy Dog, and he's as sharp as a skinning knife. Put yourself in his place: He's got his back to the wall, and now we're trying to take away the wall."

"If I'm not being inquisitive," Merritt asked drily, "whose side are you on?"

"Until the arrows begin to fly, I'm on theirs. I'm for trying to buy trail rights from them, not steal them." He felt his patience thinning for this dour man who could not understand that in the country of the red man, the white man was alien.

Dale Merritt was drawing something from a knitting bag on her lap. She was a small-waisted, red-haired girl with eyes which were actually green—glass-green—and Sam Cary remembered things he had heard about green-eyed women.

"Will you give another greenhorn some advice?" She tossed him a slightly wilted prairie blossom. "I want to know if that's what you call *kinnikinnick*."

Cary studied it in mock seriousness. "Not quite. *Kinnikinnick* is a mess of bark, leaves and dirt the Indians smoke instead of tobacco. So do I, when I can't get tobacco.''

Dale laughed. ''Asa, I've made a fool of myself. You see,'' she told Sam, ''I botanize—collect flowers. Sometimes I press them. Usually I paint them in watercolors. It's quite fashionable in the East. I'd be the talk of Washington if I could go back with a collection of genuine Wyoming wild flowers. Would you have time before it's dark tonight to point out some plants to me?''

Cary glanced quickly at the doctor, who regarded his wife in slow gravity and then gave his attention again to the laboring mules. Cary hedged. ''After the chores, if there's time. Doctor, I could show you some herbs that would match anything in your bag.''

Merritt grunted. ''For suddenness, perhaps. No, thanks.''

Dale's eyes veiled themselves momentarily as Cary looked doubtfully at her, and she smiled, ''After the chores, then.''

In mid-afternoon they reached the shell of Fort Reno, on the Dry Fork of Powder River. The gap-toothed picket walls and burned structures loomed on a sagebrush bench above the river. The sun struck brassily on aisles of muddy water between sand bars. Where the land had not been cleared, sage and lean cottonwoods fringed the river.

Cary corralled the wagons with Stockwell's on the flat ground between the old stables and the fort proper. He sent the stock to the river to be watered.

Day scouts ranged in and four horsemen rode out. At the wooden dishpan, Gaybird finished her dishes. She wore a striped dress that Sam had told her made her look like candy; it was roman-striped, full below, snug above. Wind and heat had richened her skin; her eyes were a lighter gray; her lashes darker.

Cary had been absent from their mess, but now he came up from the bosk.

". . . I'll borrow your buggy rifle for Mrs. Merritt," he said.

"What in heaven's name for?"

"Precaution. She's got it in her head to collect wild-flowers."

"Why, that's ridiculous! You wouldn't dare go far enough to find anything the stock hadn't trampled. She can find her flowers right in the corral." Gaybird's cheeks heated.

"I don't mean to get out of sight." Sam shrugged.

"I'd rather you left the rifle," Gaybird said. "The idea in giving it to me was for protection, wasn't it?" Her cheeks were flushed.

"That's right. And I'll bet if you had to, you couldn't break a vinegar jug at ten feet!"

Gaybird's chin tilted. But she was suddenly unsure what her voice might do, and she turned her back on him.

Sam laughed and strode off. But a feeling of a music box tinkling inside him stayed with him.

Dale was waiting when he arrived at the ambulance. The doctor was off at his evening chores, pulling aching teeth and puncturing boils.

They moved down the meagre slope to the stream. A scout loafed out westward, the tail of his pony streaming. A shoulder of cottonweeds bent the stream. They rounded it and Cary halted to pick a blossom.

"Evening star," he said. "Scarce, down here."

She turned it in her fingers. "Then I may as well start with it. I like things that are scarce."

"Mrs. Merritt," Sam said, "you talk like a prophet sometimes. In parables."

"That's almost the only way a woman can talk, isn't it?"

He dipped a cup of water for her colors and gathered a small bunch of flowers. She began to sketch. Cary sat against a rock to smoke. He was impressed with the strangeness of her being the wife of a dry-minded man like Merritt.

"Do you like being a trader, Sam?" she asked suddenly.

"If I didn't, I wouldn't be one."

"Still, you'll have to admit there are disadvantages to your life."

"Just one," Cary declared: "Sometimes I have to go into town."

"One thing you must miss. Women."

He shrugged. "Something else you can get used to doing without, like whiskey."

"Tell me something," Dale said. "Are you in love with Gay?"

Cary looked into his pipe. "She's just a child, isn't she?"

"A beautiful and mischievous child. I think she's playing you against Mark Stockwell."

"Gaybird happens to be my partner, not my fiancee."

"I don't mean to intrude in anything you don't want me to," Dale said. "We'll talk about something else, if you'd rather. We'll talk about how wrong women can be. I was wrong about being a country doctor's wife. It looked dramatic, to a girl who didn't like being a grocer's daughter. But there's less drama to it than there is penny-pinching!"

"Then I was wrong about being a diplomat's wife. I made Asa take this political job, through a friend who went to Washington. But we landed in a Mexican desert town, instead of in Paris. And now we're in the middle of nowhere. In fact, this is the closest thing to excitement I've had yet!"

"I'd say we'd had more dust than excitement."

"Does excitement always have to mean Indians?"

"Mrs. Merritt," Cary sighed, "you're talking in parables again."

Smiling, she looked down at her sketch. "This is

really one of the nicest specimens of wild-life I've done.''

It was not professional work, but it was skilled amateur. The colors were deep brown, rose and white against the green of mountain ash. The face was his own—long, hard-fleshed, dark. He took it from her, thinking sadly of that somnolent man who was her husband. He slowly tore the page twice, dropping it on the ground.

''That wasn't very mannerly, Sam,'' Dale said crisply. ''What did you think I meant by it?''

''I don't know. I can guess what the doctor would think.''

Suddenly a change entered her face, a rush of apprehension. Cary heard the slow tread of boots. The lean form of the doctor came into view. Dale picked up the stool quickly and started toward him. Cary followed her.

''Find what you wanted?'' Merritt asked.

''I made a wretched job of it,'' Dale shrugged. ''Coming back with me?''

''No. I'll stretch my legs a bit.''

''Better make it quick,'' Cary advised him.

Dale took her husband's arm. ''Sam's right, Asa. Don't worry me by wandering about.''

Merritt patted her hand. ''Never worry over any man,'' he smiled. ''It puts lines in a woman's face. And then—who knows?—perhaps she can't get another!''

Dale said, ''Do hurry, then,'' and walked on.

Merritt watched them, his wife and the trader, a slender feminine form and a lanky masculine shape. Twenty years ago, he thought, I'd have outweighed him. But this was not twenty years ago. This was tonight, and Dale's eyes were so guileless he was certain they hid a deeper guile than any she had yet shown him. He proceeded to the point where the rumpled earth showed him they had stopped.

He was ashamed of his suspicions, but he could not

take his eyes from the ground. He saw where she had sat, the feet of the camp stool plain in the ground. He found, by heel-marks and a small rubble of burned tobacco, where Cary had sat.

Then he saw the torn sheet of drawing paper. Curious, he picked it up. It was no trouble to fit the pieces together. He regarded Cary's features without changing expression. His hands slowly made a packet of the drawing paper and he slipped it into his pocket.

He stood that way, his eyes lost in bitter reverie, until a falling pebble startled him. He faced around, half-frightened, his head full of the Indian tales the whackers told one another. A whistler squirrel popped into a hole.

His face somber, he started slowly back to the wagon camp.

4

Judas of the Wagon Trail

OUT OF THE BADLANDS A WIND CAME TO HISS OVER the rabbit brush and whip hot sand through the wagons. For two days the wagons groaned across the hot current of it. One morning they discovered the ghost-like outline of the Bighorns of the northwest. At Crazy Woman's Fork of the Powder they lumbered through a wide alley of alkali water and sandbars. In two days they would make the transition from desert to pines.

By process of rotation, Bill Orrum had worked up to the head of the wagon train. He would have felt safer traveling with a riding mule and a pack-animal than in this lumbering company of bullwhackers.

His only compulsion was to sell the wagonload of ancient smoothbore muskets he carried, and he began to be impatient to make a deal short of Montana. The rifles weighted him like an anchor, but Stockwell was still evasive about closing with him.

It seemed timely that the trader should jog by the

wagon this mid-afternoon with his hat tugged down against the cold north wind and his carbine slanted across his saddle. Stockwell's eyes were on the foothills ten miles west. He was staring attentively when the gun-runner said, "Got a minute, Mark?"

Stockwell looked around. "No more than that. There's a herd of antelope over yonder. I'm one trader that's had a bellyful of jerky."

The mules humping up a long slope, Orrum struck a match for his pipe. "I wouldn't rush into a hunt in these hills, Mark. You rushed into trading about the same way though, didn't you?"

"No. Who told you I did?"

"A man that braces an old-timer like Cary is either a greenhorn or an optimist."

"I thought I'd done pretty well. The cash book's fat enough."

Orrum saw ill-nature darkening Stockwell's face. "You know how it seems to me? Merritt's the man you want to worry about. Not Cary."

"How's that?"

"You get fat on trouble, Mark. Cary gets fat on peace. Merritt's a peace-maker."

A hard smile shaped Stockwell's mouth. "What kind of a peacemaker?"

"He's got a good teacher. Cary aims to help him make a treaty, too. Then where'll you be?"

Stockwell said, "I don't think I've got much to worry about. Esconella's promised scalps and powder to half the tribes in Wyoming. Crazy Dog is finished as a chief."

"Be a good idea to know how you stand with Esconella, anyhow. There ain't nothing that tickles an Injun like a new rifle. And them rebel Sioux are going to need guns if they tackle a log-walled post. I could be talked out of these I'm carrying, I reckon."

Orrum saw the same expression in Mark Stockwell's eyes which he had seen in Cary's the day he paid him for the guns. He wondered what made a man think he was any better than the men he traded with.

"It hasn't come to that, yet, and I hope it won't."

He swung his horse away, but heard Orrum remark, "From now until we hit Fort Graybull, there'll be Injun eyes on us every hour of the day. There was fifteen hundred that cleaned out Fetterman. I wonder how many'll hit us? If you want to make a trade with them, Mark, make it soon."

The wind wrestled with the wagons as they sidled from the backbone of the ridge into the bosk of a creek. Cary shouted them into formation on the stream bank. While he was finishing this chore he saw Mark Stockwell riding in; he had not seen Stockwell since he took off three hours earlier to hunt antelope. It was a few minutes later that Silvertooth came after him. The wagonmaster's sand-scoured face was lined.

"Come over here," Silvertooth said shortly.

Stockwell stood with a half-dozen bullwhackers and Coy Mullan in the lee of a freight-trailer. Conversation halted as the men approached.

Silvertooth, breathing deeply, said, "Tell him about your Injun, Stockwell."

Something in Cary tightened.

His face ruddy, Stockwell said, "I had to kill an Indian out there. We nearly bumped into each other, hunting. I happened to drop him first."

Cary swung at the trader's head. Stockwell went down among the boots of the teamsters, Cary lunging after him. But Silvertooth was there to pin Cary against a wagon, and suddenly bullwhackers were piling onto both men to separate them.

The blood slowly left Cary's head. He said, "So you killed a buck. We were within aces of making a treaty to open this country up again. And you had to kill a Sioux."

"It's always open season on us," Stockwell snapped,

"but I have to let them take first crack at me: Is that it?"

"He was hunting antelope, not traders, or he wouldn't have been alone."

Silvertooth growled, "Well, it's done. We'll know in a day or two how much harm's been done. Where'd you leave him?"

"In a wash."

After a moment Cary said, "Donovan, go get Doctor Merritt. It's time Stockwell and I had a talk with him."

Donovan returned with the envoy. The doctor's face was raw with sanding, his eyes black and dull as nail-heads. He demanded, "What's more important than my finishing my supper in peace, Cary?"

"Finishing the trip in peace. You wanted to meet Crazy Dog? Well, you're about to have the opportunity. We're leaving for the village tomorrow."

Cary waited for his dignified hedging, while Silver-tooth swore under his breath and the other men stirred in surprise. But after a moment's thought the doctor said, "You mean we'd go up alone, without escort?"

"It doesn't take a troop of cavalry to carry an olive branch."

The envoy's dark eyes crinkled. "Well, why not? The kill or cure treatment for Indian troubles, eh? I'll be ready."

Cary turned to Stockwell. "In the meantime, you can make up a pack-load of trade goods. Don't skimp. I'll present them to Crazy Dog and tell him about your buck before he catches his breath. It's the only way I know of to handle it. You might throw in that ring you're wearing, as a token of mourning . . ."

An hour after sun-up, Cary, Doctor Merritt and Don-ovan left the train. Silvertooth put the wagons back on the road for the fort. Whips and leather lungs snapped the line into shape, scouts ranged distantly, and the dogged monotony of the trail settled again as chokingly as the dust.

Bill Orrum tooled his wagons into the train. He was in the cloud of earthy smoke at the rear when Mark Stockwell pulled in beside him. Stockwell handled his horse cavalierly. Of his features, masked against the dust, only his eyes were revealed.

"Still think you'll try it alone, eh?" Stockwell inquired.

"Bound to. I aim to drop out of the train. I know a shortcut through the foothills. I'll be in Butte before you're at Fort Stockwell. I'd like to be heeled when I get there, too. These customers of mine, now, don't always pay in cash money."

Stockwell put a slip of paper into the gun-runner's hand. "Give that to my manager at the fort."

Orrum tucked it into the sweat-band of his hat. "Thanks, Mark. May seem steep, but think of the risks."

"You're right it's steep. Smooth-bore muskets for the price of Spencers! That's Cherry Spring, now? Don't be in any rush to close in with Esconella. I'd like to clear Fort Graybull and be heading up into my own country before the bucks get the guns out of the grease. Stall them for a while, if you can. This is close timing."

They gripped hands briefly. Orrum pulled his wagon out of line and pointed it northwest.

That night, with twelve miles behind them, Cary camped on a green meadow, under fragrant pines. In the morning, he and Donovan talked it over.

"We should make the village before night, if they haven't moved," Cary declared. "As an infantryman, what's your opinion of how we should proceed?"

"Backwards," said Donovan. "At least, I'm with the men this time. Did you need somebody to wash the pots?"

"If you've been bragging about the kind of soldiering you did," said Cary, "I'll take your scalp myself."

They penetrated a flinty highland of sparse timber and bleached grasses. A buzzard tilted overhead. On a cold rim of granite, Donovan put his pony across the ridge to protect their flank. Cary loafed along the trail.

Presently, Merritt called, "Will you stop at the next stream? I'm dry."

Cary swung down at a spring branch and let his horse drink. He stretched, looked about him, and knelt to scoop water in the brim of his hat. The doctor dismounted. When Cary looked up, hatbrim to his lips, he saw Merritt standing there silently with a pistol in his hand. The gun was directed at Cary's belly.

Cary let the water spill. "What's this?"

"This," said Merritt, "is the wages of sin. Was she worth it, Cary?"

The pure logic of it overwhelmed Cary. Merritt, contradicting everything he knew about the man, to endorse this sortie!

"Was she worth it?" Cary repeated. "I wouldn't know. I just wouldn't know."

He began to rise, but Merritt snapped, "You'd better stay down."

"On my knees?"

The doctor was all resolution and suppressed fury, which he seemed trying to liberate. "Would you like to tell me about the night at Fort Reno?"

Cary shrugged. "I didn't know she was painting my picture, Merritt. But if she was painting, she didn't have time to get into any other mischief, did she?"

"You were gone close to an hour." His hand trembled. "I don't like this any better than you do. A doctor gets used to trying to save lives. But I'm a man first and a doctor afterward."

"From what I've seen of doctors, I'd rather have one operate on me with a Colt."

"If you're going to die protecting the lady's name, then—"

"This is a damn shame," Cary sighed. "It's a shame for the white traders and the Sioux. There's nothing between them and war, now. And it's a shame for you, because you won't get back. And," he sighed again, "I'm sorry for my wife, too."

"Your wife?"

"Gaybird. We've been married for four years. It was a sort of guardianship, after her father died. But it's been—well, subject to annulment, up to now. I was thinking it wouldn't be, by fall."

Merritt's fault, as a killer, was that he was amenable to logic. Sam saw him flashing back over the whole month on the trail. "She wears no ring," he stated.

"It wasn't meant to be a marriage. But the fact is— Dammit," he said, "it's none of your business what's between us."

Merritt took a long, steadying breath. "It might be."

Cary peered into the intent features. "I think she thought she loved me. But that was in Cheyenne, and I still figured she was a kid, and felt obligated to me."

"I thought I detected a certain amount of affection between you," Merritt observed.

Cary wagged his head. "Of all the men to confuse affection and love, Doctor, you ought to be the last."

"Where does one begin and the other end?" Merritt scoffed.

"They're two different things. I think when Dale married you she had affection for you. But she happened to be in love with you, too, and now that the affection is gone, all that's left is love."

Merritt's bitter smile came. "How did you arrive at the conclusion that my wife had anything but contempt for me?"

"No one," Cary said, "will ever have contempt for you. People may hate you, but you've got a sort of bedside manner that lets you take over in a situation.

Yet you've kept Dale at arm's-length so long that her eyes have begun to stray.''

''Will you give me one inkling of her love for me?'' Merritt challenged.

''Sure. The fact that she's in Wyoming. She knew it was dangerous, and yet she came with you. If she'd wanted to play it fast and loose, she'd have stayed in Washington.''

Merritt's face weighed it. It silenced him.

''People ought to stick to what they're good at,'' Cary said. ''You were a good doctor. But you threw it up to be a second-rate politician. And now that you're in a bind, do you know the one thing that's apt to get you out? Medicine. You're going to work on old Crazy Dog!''

Merritt shuddered. ''Man, there are seven thousand things that can cause paralysis of the limbs! One or two of them are susceptible to treatment.''

''But this was the result of a shot. I thought maybe— Well, it's a chance.''

''You thought maybe I was God,'' Merritt grunted.

''I had a doctor staying at the post one winter,'' Cary said. ''He worked on dozens of Indians. If there's a living god, to them, it's a man with a brown cowhide bag. Put yourself in Crazy Dog's place. A man comes all the way from Washington, not to make a treaty, but to make him well. The white man's medicine brings the chief some relief. Maybe it cures him. Then, Doctor, he begins talking peace terms!''

There was a loosening look about Merritt.

''Women are pretty strong medicine themselves,'' Cary smiled. ''You need to be your own man when you go to dickering with them. That's been your mistake. Dale let you doubt yourself. Don't. Not for *any* woman.''

The gun dangled in the physician's hand. He said, ''And I had to travel two thousand miles to find a man who talked this good sense! Do I go back in irons, or do we go on?''

''We go on.'' Cary watched him turn away to pick up the reins of his horse, and he took the drink he had spilled before, and then walked to his own pony. He took a moment, before mounting, to wipe his palms carefully on his buckskin thighs. The perspiration made dark prints on the smoked leather.

The climb stiffened. There became increasing evidence that they were in someone's dooryard—someone who left shards of old pottery about, bright scatters of arrow-chips, bleached bones of buffalo.

And now a horse clattered on the ridge, and a rider let his horse tumble down the slope. Donovan was plunging in with his tough features ropy with fear.

''In that tamarack, Cary! A platoon of the varmints, a-hossback and waiting!''

Cary squinted at the dark-green cones of timber masking the mouth of a canyon which funneled in between two hills. ''All right,'' he said. ''That's what we've been waiting for, isn't it?'' He lifted his right hand and jogged toward the trees.

There was a flutter of color and something arched from the trees. It spun and twisted in the cold mountain sunlight and struck the ground ahead of Cary. The feathered arrow-shaft slowly fell over. Cary halted, his belly-muscles wadding. Everything had been a prelude to this instant, and now no man knew how the next few moments would go.

From the trees the Indians began to file, Sioux soldiers, toughened and tamed by experience. Cary looked for Crazy Dog. The chief was not in the party, but Cary saw his son, Yellow Horn.

The Sioux drew up, robed and belted, bright with ornament. Cary raised his hand again.

''How is my friend, Yellow Horn?'' he greeted, in Ogallala.

The Ogallala studied him. "How is it that you come?"

"The grandfather sends us. We come as an old friend and as a new one."

"What does the grandfather wish? More buffalo to steal?"

The Sioux ringed them tightly. A brave thumped the rawhide *aparejo* straddling the packhorse which carried food and gifts.

"We bring presents," Cary declared. "We bring the greatest medicine man the white man knows."

They stared at Donovan and then came close to Merritt, gaping and pulling at his brown cowhide bag. He flinched but Cary said casually, "Easy."

After a moment Yellow Horn said, "Can he cure sick legs?"

"Maybeso Crazy Dog walks again."

Yellow Horn nodded slowly. "You come," he said.

Beyond the trees a trail lifted them to a hillside which sloughed off into a wide valley. Smokes rose lazily from many fires. It was like entering a vast and untidy fairground, only instead of tents there were hundreds of tepees scattered randomly. Dogs nosed about, yapping at them. Babies squalled and squaws gathered in groups and screeched at naked boys to keep back from the Long Knives. Hides were pegged on the ground under stirring mantles of flies. Yellow Horn stopped once and pointed at a fat white mongrel dog, and a squaw laid hold of it swiftly and struck it on the head with a rock. She dragged it, twitching, away to a fire.

Merritt's face sickened. "Are we—expected to eat—"

Cary grinned. "Best sign in the world. A dog-feast."

Before a lodge where a bullhide shield hung on a tripod, Yellow Horse slipped from his pony. He ducked inside, and presently came back to summon two warriors. They carried the paralyzed chief out. He wore a bronze treaty medal on a rawhide cord about his neck. Weight had sloughed off his stocky frame since Cary saw him last. A white buffalo robe was belted about his middle and his heavy, plaited braids came forward across his shoulders. His face was wrinkled bronze with glints of black Indian eyes.

Cary spoke briefly with the chief. From his pocket he took the ruby ring of Stockwell's. Sitting propped against a boulder, Crazy Dog smiled and slipped it onto his finger.

"Long Rifle does not come to his friends often," he said.

"A trader is busy."

"Yellow Horn says the grandfather sends his medicine man to cure me."

Cary put a hand on Merritt's shoulder. "He has cured many white chiefs. Maybeso his medicine cures you."

"We will go inside."

The lodge was stifling with its rancid-sweat odors of hides and sweat and food. The chief mixed tobacco, lighted a pipe and passed it. Between silences, there was talk. Then the elders rose again and all but Yellow Horn, another Ogallala, and the chief left the tepee.

Cary turned to the physician. "All right, Doctor. This is your big play. He's your patient."

Merritt asked the chief to have the fire built up so that he could see better. He said to Cary, "Can he tell me anything about this?"

"He was shot in a hunting accident. We'll say it was an accident. He hasn't walked since."

Merritt sighed. He helped the chief turn over on his face and removed the belted robe. The firelight glistened on skin like discolored brown metal. He touched a large scar on the man's spine. Cary heard the doctor murmur. He bent over, his fingers prodding gently at Crazy Dog's back. He sat back.

"What is it?" Cary asked.

"I'm not sure. I would say he has either a large concretion alongside his spine, or the bullet is still there. But either way . . . I don't know."

Yellow Horn spoke to Cary. "He says the medicine men thought there was a bullet in him," Cary translated, "and they burned cow-dung over the wound to drive it out. But nothing happened."

"Surprising," Merritt remarked. His face was glum in the warm firelight. He groped in his bag and dispensed sulphate of morphia. Suddenly he smiled. "Nervous?" he asked Cary.

"Passably."

"You should be."

"Why?"

"Because we're working on ten-to-one odds. But there's always that tenth chance."

Suddenly Donovan growled. "Here comes that squaw with a kettle! Have we got to eat that damned dog?"

"You'd pick a fight with a man who wouldn't drink with you, wouldn't you?"

Crazy Dog sat up again. They ate the dog stew. Accustomed to Indian delicacies, Cary was able to eat his share. Presently, as the morphine took effect, Merritt prepared to work. "I have candles here," he said. "Will you men hold them?"

The operation was brief. The chief grunted occasionally. Merritt carefully laid on a handkerchief a lead ball. He bluestoned the wound and fixed a dressing over it.

"All right," he said. "Let's take him outside."

Cary watched the warriors place the chief on the buffalo robe before the lodge. A staring pack of squaws, braves and children had collected. They spoke in soft, low rushes. Shell ornaments rattled and moccasins whispered on the bare earth. Merritt eyed them uneasily.

"If they're waiting for a miracle," he said, "they're going to be disappointed. After three months, it's hardly to be expected that he should take up his bed and walk. It will take some time."

"How much time?"

"Days . . . weeks. I don't know. I should think, perhaps, only a few days."

"But by fall for sure?"

"In time for the treaty commission?" Merritt smiled. "Yes. He'll walk by then, if he walks at all."

In the watchful silence, Cary brought the rawhide packs containing the gifts. On a blanket he set out dusky hanks of tobacco, bolts of red cotton, papers of needles and spools of thread. He produced a large silver watch and demonstrated it. Crazy Dog put the watch under his robe, his eyes gleaming. It was when he moved to do this that Merritt spoke suddenly.

"There's our sign, Cary."

In moving, the Indian had spread his legs slightly and again drawn them together. Cary had noticed this without being impressed. But now the doctor said quickly:

"Ask him to bend his knees."

Cary translated. His back to the smoky boulder beside his shield-rack, Crazy Dog placed his palms on the robe. His knees bent and rose four or five inches off the robe. Yellow Horn said something in a deep, excited voice. The dark eyes of the Sioux came to Merritt.

"Tell them," Merritt said, "he'll be able to walk within two weeks."

Cary let the moment stretch out, tightening, before he announced, "In the time of the full moon, your chief will walk from his lodge to the river. When leaves fall, he will lead the hunt."

There was a great noise of Indian voices, the tribe breaking. The old chief's smile squinted his face and he beckoned to the doctor. Merritt squatted beside him. Removing his necklace of bearclaws, the Ogallala placed it about the doctor's neck. He spoke to Cary.

"He says you're the greatest healer the Sioux Nation has ever seen," Cary grinned. "He wants you to treat all of his people who are sick. That would mean about ninety per cent of them. If you were ever looking prestige in the eye, Merritt, it's right now.''

Merritt looked about. Cary had the sudden fear that he would back out: That the smell and filth of the diseased would be too much for him. But a look of deep calm came to Merritt's face.

''You were right,'' he declared. ''A man ought to stick with what he's good at. . . . Tell them to go to their lodges. I'll visit them all in turn.''

Merritt started his grand tour of the lodges, and Cary eased into his own business. He sat in the stuffy deerskin lodge with the chief and his old men.

''The medicine man was from the grandfather,'' he told Crazy Dog. ''The gifts were from the trader, Stockwell.''

Quick, dark eyes were on Cary, keen as fleshing knives. ''Owns Lance is not our friend. Why does he send gifts?''

''Owns Lance wishes to be your friend. He sends the gifts in grief, because he killed one of your young men. It was by accident.''

Crazy Dog's breath sounded lightly between his teeth. ''Owns Lance does nothing by accident. We thought Loud Bear died in the big wind. Why did he kill him? Has Owns Lance a sickness?''

''He was afraid. He saw him in the wind and killed him before he thought.''

''Why did he not bring the gifts himself?''

''Because he was afraid. Esconella has frightened many of the traders.''

Crazy Dog shook his head. ''The heart has gone bad in him. He has left the village of his fathers. He has four hundred men with him and he will find more. He has sent presents to the Brules and Uncpapas. The whole village of Two Elks has gone with him.''

''But Crazy Dog is still chief.''

The Ogallala peered at him. ''Crazy Dog is chief, as there is fire in flint. But first it must be struck. Without legs I cannot strike fire. If the white man's medicine is strong, Esconella will play with the boys again."

"If he comes back," Cary asked, "can you handle him?"

"He will not come back. He has sent my daughter back to my lodge. He has laughed at the Wind God. He is stubborn and stiffnecked. If he steals guns, he will be dangerous."

"If he does not steal guns, and the tribes do not take the warpath, will you talk peace with the white soldiers?"

The chief received it stolidly. "Why do they want to talk peace, when they will not keep peace? When they still steal?"

"They are sorry for the acts of white liars and thieves. They want to repay you for the buffalo they have slaughtered and the warriors that they have killed."

"What is it they want?" Crazy Dog asked sharply.

"They wish to man the Bozeman posts again. To police traders and travelers, as well as renegade Indians."

"Will they pay for this?"

"They will pay."

Crazy Dog spoke to one of the Indians. In the lodge there was a thin strand of conversation, a word grunted, a sign made. At last he told Cary, "We will make no promises. But we will talk when the leaves fall. If Crazy Dog is still chief of the Ogallalas."

Night came before Merritt was finished. Cary noticed that the Indians kept sentries out. Esconella had left nothing with his tribe but the fear of him. Cary, Donovan and the doctor spread their blankets outside Crazy Dog's lodge. Silence came. Mountain cold pressed sharply upon them. Small fires puddled the dark ground, expiring into coals; dogs relinquished their yapping and the last child ceased to complain. The camp slept.

Cary lay with his fingers laced under his head. He pictured the wagons forted up tonight on the lap of Red's Meadow. At noon tomorrow they would ford Silvertip

Creek, and before nightfall they would make Fort Graybull, on Young Woman Creek. Cary himself hoped to
make it by dark.

From the blankets at his side, Merritt's voice came
with the solemnity of a sleep-talker.

"It's here, Cary. It's all right here. They sent me out
to make a fool of myself. Wyoming—the graveyard of
diplomats. But I didn't make a fool of myself. By God,
I didn't!"

With a guide and a pack-horse-load of gifts, they left
the village at sunup.

Working down from the crests, their guide took them
through a swift descent, finally pulling up on a timbered
ridge above the grassy foothills. He pointed with his
rifle.

"Half day ride." The gun barrel swerved southward.
"Whackers sleepin' late!"

Cary studied a pencil of smoke rising from the hills.
"No," he said. "My men would be nooning on Silvertip by now. Maybeso Esconella?"

"Esconella rides north to meet Brules and Uncpapas."

"What's the varmint say?" Donovan demanded.

"He says that the smoke yonder is our camp. He says
it can't be Esconella, because he's north of here, waiting for the Brules."

"Are they going to spoil their record about never
laying siege to a fort?"

"They've never finished one."

The guide riding back, they followed a canyon onto
a grassy apron. As they drew near the smoke, it became
a meaningless smear, a grassy smudge against the sky.
They angled up a grassy ridge, and Donovan precipi-
tously crowded past, eager and curious. They saw him
pull up on the crest, staring down. He did not turn nor
signal, but as they came abreast of him they saw the

burned wagons and dead bulls below them, on a spring branch called Cherry Creek.

The camp was on the bank of the creek, a trampled acre of bruised grass and broken brush. In the center of this area of rubbish and hoofmarks lay the remnants of a single wagon and trailer. The wagons had long ago burned out, but the smoke of foodstuffs and robes fumed in the wreckage. Arrows pin-cushioned the oxen.

They found the bullwhacker had been pinned to the ground with stakes through his wrists. Skilled, curious knives had been at his body. The corners of his mouth had been gashed and his nose was cut off. His moccasins were on his feet but his leather breeches had been cut away in several places.

How he had died, from which wound or from sheer pain, no one could have said. He was unrecognizable, but they had lived a month with that round-crowned Stetson, with the greasy buckskins and the quilled leather shirt, and they knew them instantly for trader Bill Orrum's. Nothing was missing but his black pigtails.

Everywhere lay remnants of gun-chests and ammunition cases, split yellow-pine slabs stenciled in black. A few paper cartridges lay about. Using a board as a shovel, Cary scooped out a shallow grave and Donovan dragged the gaunt body into the trench. Cary secured his clothing, dropping the Stetson with its greasy sweatband across the mutilated face, the deerhide breeches across the hips. He held the Blackfoot shirt in his hands.

Paper whispered in a pocket. Cary pulled out a fold of writing.

Mr. Williams: Please give bearer two thousand dollars in gold, for value received. Stockwell.

"For value received," Cary said. He and Donovan gazed at each other, and Donovan's face broke oddly.

"Damn it, Cary!" he said. "Esconella's got his guns!"

"He's got the guns," Cary said. "All he needs now is the guts."

5

Blockhouse of Damnation

SILVERTOOTH POKED ALONG AT THE HEAD OF THE
column, slapping at flies on the neck of his mule. They
were in the meadow country, at last; the green country,
the country of oceans of grass and islands of pine, of
water you could drink without straining and grass that
didn't crackle when you walked on it.

They had spent the night in Red's Meadow, that un-
believable park just a few miles from the desert. Then
they had strung out again, nooned on Silvertip Creek
and this late afternoon were working down through
piney hills to the pale-green valley of Young Woman
Creek, the blue-black mountains at their back.

Silvertooth, never getting far from Gaybird's wagon,
carried a worry or two. Last night Mark Stockwell had
pulled out with his wagons. He was taking the shortcut
which lopped off a few miles but denied him the comfort of a day or two in Fort Graybull before the last fifty

miles of his own trip. Bill Orrum had left earlier in the
day on another cut-off. Their behavior puzzled him.

From a high tuck in the hills, they had their first view
of the fort.

It was a half-hour distant, still. Fenced by sharpened
lodgepole logs, the buildings looked trim as match
boxes. Silvertooth waved the word down the line and
loped out to look for his scouts. He had a treacherous
desire to let down. He wanted to signal them all in:
We're done, boys, draw your pay and spend it!

But he had been through too much on the Bozeman
to be fooled.

After a time he saw Tom Kane, one of the scouts,
sloping in from the north. Another rider suddenly
slashed up from a coulee just behind Kane, and Silvertooth's heart squeezed. But it was not a Sioux: After a
brief conference, the pair came in at a hard lope. Silvertooth waited.

The man with Kane was Coy Mullan. As they reined
in on the green, granite-ribboned hillside, Silvertooth
saw that the wagon-master's features were ashen. He
rode with his revolver in his hand. He was out of breath.
He waved the gun pointlessly and gasped, "Damn the
varmints! Damn them!"

Silvertooth struck the gun aside. "What's the trouble,
now?"

Mullan stared with a sick fear. "One of the scouts
flushed Esconella and a whole gad-blamed army in a
coulee, waitin' for us! We've turned back. Got three-
four miles, maybe, but they're ramping down on the
train like the devil splitting kindling! Mark's bringing
the wagon back to the fort. We're a mile and a half
north, in the creek bottom."

Silvertooth turned to fire a shot and bawl a warning.
An outrider snapped his arm back and forth, turned and
ran his horse at the train. By standing in the stirrups,
Silvertooth was able to discern a dirty-gray flow of canvas sheets in the bosk of Young Woman Creek. It was

the Montana train, slicing back to the post. He shuddered at the thought of the gigantic log-jam of wagons crowding through the sally-port at once.

He groaned then, and turned, and that was when he saw three horsemen sliding down a hill a mile to the rear. But these riders came like whites, bent low across their saddle-swells.

A hosanna went up from Silvertooth's lips. Sam . . . Sam and Donovan and the doctor. Triumphantly he bore down on the train, no longer an old woman fussing with trivialities, but feeling himself growing.

They met at the rear and Silvertooth started to pass the word.

"We saw them from the hills," Cary interrupted. "They've got the guns Orrum was carrying. Orrum's been murdered. Better cut loose the heavy wagons and bring the rest in. Merritt and I will take the women to the fort."

With an instinct for emergency, Cary had left the arms-wagon only half-loaded. He whipped it out of line with its four span of strong young mules and sent it on. He drafted a hunter to take Gaybird's wagon in, and put her on his horse behind him. Her skirts billowed at either side of the horse. As they rode, he glanced back. "You don't have to squeeze the wind out of me. I won't leave you."

She squeezed harder, closing her eyes. Never, never, her lips said.

They came off the last hill into the wide and indolent valley of Young Woman Creek. Near the western margin of it ran the creek in its entourage of cottonwoods and silver aspen, tender with new leaves. Hunters' trails ran down to a sandy ford about a half mile from the post walls. Marks of travois scarred the meadow and hillsides, where Indian potato and wild onion had been dug. At the back of the fort rose a small hill capped by a high lookout tower. Beyond the hill was a reach of two miles of meadow, and then the hills again, stiff with timber.

They threaded the road through the trees, feeling the moist coolness of the bosk. Berry thickets crowded close to the road and wild hop festooned the cotton-woods. They plunged through the stream. Silver spray drenched them. Gaybird's skirts ceased to billow; they modeled her legs glisteningly.

Shading his hand, Cary peered northwest. He made out the Montana train lunging back to the fort. Beyond, on the slope of a distant hill, he discerned a blur of moving horses.

As they left the trees, Cary's post manager, Daniel Edge, came in sight beyond the haystacks. A two-hundred-and-fifty-pound man whose body turned everything he ate into fat, Edge swung his horse in beside them.

"A hell of a homecoming!" he shouted, his brown eyes vehement.

"You know about the Sioux?"

"The lookout spotted them. He made them at seven-eight hundred. I've got all the men on the walls."

"How many around?"

"Maybe forty."

For round numbers, Cary reckoned, a hundred inside the post if the wagons made it in, seven to eight hundred without.

They loped past the haystacks and outer corral. They crossed the mauled ground about the main gate. A square blockhouse dominated the northwest corner of the post, matched by a similar barn-like structure on the southeast. From loopholes in the blockhouse and along the walls, men were shouting at them. The tall gate made a two-foot slot. They crowded into the narrow, walled passage, where Indians were penned for trading in uncertain times. A sentry bawled and the inner gate grudgingly opened. They entered the post.

Cary felt Gaybird's arms relax. He heard her sigh. He explained it, too—the comfort of the walls.

The great, engulfing ocean of the wilderness could not break through the slim dike of sharpened poles. This square, no larger than a town block, had a cramped-down strength of many towns. It was a strong mix of abilities, cunning and courage. Whoever broke that dike would not only let the wilderness pour in but would release a barbarous energy on himself.

Across two-thirds of the enclosure fell the notched shadow of the forward wall. Log and rock buildings occupied the area to the right; the remaining space was an emergency corral filled with stock. Drenched and windblown, Gaybird held to the stirrup as Sam lowered her. Cary faced Dan Edge. "Get the women settled. Then get on the wall. If Stockwell beats me to the gate, hold him off. If the Sioux beat us both, lock the gates. We'll stand them off outside. We've all the rifles we can use, if it comes to a showdown. Trapdoor Springfields! You'll hear 'em.''

Edge ducked his chin to his shoulder to wipe a droplet of sweat. Gaybird touched Sam's hand as he moved to ride out. "Sam! I keep thinking—if anything should happen—would we have to spend eternity in a sort of purgatory?''

Cary smiled. "Gaybird,'' he sighed, "I've been in purgatory. Whatever happens, one way or another, I'm coming out of it. Be a good girl and go along with Dan. Mrs. Merritt will join you. You can't have a light, but I reckon you can pray in the dark.''

Wheels echoed hollowly in the sallyport and the Merritts rattled in. Cary struck the horse with his hat and went through the gate.

Northwest, across the cropped meadow, he quietly observed Stockwell's wagons muling through the upper ford. Spray splashed silver in the sunlight. A wagon was bogged in sand and the skinner was wallowing ashore to catch a ride. All the commotion of a full-scale retreat was there, teamsters standing to rawhide stumbling mules, freight sprawling out of lurching wagons, hubs grinding together as the wagons bickered for position.

Cary brought his gaze down the timbered stream-bed to where Silvertooth was dispatching the first of the Graybull wagons through the water. The wagonmaster lingered in the shallows, swinging his carbine.

Cary tried to measure the situation, but he could not reckon which train would reach the post first. A vermilion flake of color twisted in the light on a near ridge, trembling like a dead sumac leaf. He knew it for a whirled blanket, counterpart of the white soldier's trumpet. Around it swirled a wave of acorn brown, blotting the young grass. The wave widened and swept forward, punctured with glints of steel—steel which had been files and dutch ovens until squaw-cleverness fashioned lance tips from it; browned and blued steel molded in Eastern factories for savage hands to master.

He sat rubbing the breech of his gun, waiting.

It grew evident that his wagons were going to have the edge at the gate. Rambling and broken, Stockwell's gaunt line straggled across the meadow. The vanguard of Silvertooth's disciplined column was already passing the haystacks. Cary took the coiled bullwhip from his pommel and moved out before the gate.

The wave of Sioux, offscrapings of four tribes, had dimension now. It was a cloud painted gorgeously with red horsehide, with gray, green and vermilion blankets and buffalo-hide shields. A gigantic thunder cloud to drench with its fury the wagons about to jam the gate of the trading post.

Cary moved forward. He and Silvertooth met briefly. "Take them in," Cary ordered. "Straight down the line till you hit the back wall. A jam will finish us, sure as hell!"

There was a low, grinding echo of hubs from the passage as the first wagon went in. Up on the wall they were bawling encouragement. Team after team, heads low and swinging, the oxen streamed into the post.

The first of Stockwell's wagons rambled up, driven by a wild-eyed skinner with a tawny beard, a standing, shirtless figure hurling his whip. Cary moved into the way of the mules. "Turn them!" he shouted.

The skinner's wide eyes stared. He lashed the mules again.

Cary hurled the whip against a leader's neck. The cracker drew blood; the mule lumbered against its collar-mate, and he gave it the whip again. The team fell away as the muleskinner shouted and jumped down.

Stockwell came loping along the line of wagons to plunge to a halt beside Cary. His face was crusted with dirt and sweat. "They're on us, man! I had to leave some of my wagons in the creek. For God's sake, keep them moving!"

"Line them up before the gate," Cary said. "They'll serve as a final firing line."

Stockwell seized his shirt-front. "You aren't God Almighty! They can all go in, one and one."

Then he was looking at the paper Sam took from the bleached ribbon of his Stetson. His eyes rushed back to Cary's face, a stark questioning in them. He knew then what had happened to Bill Orrum, and where Cary had found the paper.

"Bring your wagons around and overturn them," Cary told him.

Stockwell raised his hand in a half-gesture of protest, but let it fall. He jerked his head at Mullan and they swung back to take over the wagons. Cary retreated to the gate.

Wagon after wagon, they jounced on. If a man focused on them, he could forget that half-a-nation of Sioux were streaming upon the post. It was a picture Cary would never forget. He would always remember how their horses stifled the bright little stream, and how the horde of them shook out over the meadow like an

Indian blanket. He would remember the broken whooping as their hands slapped their mouths. He would remember the way eight hundred running horses jarred the ground, the sensation that he was standing beneath a cliff, waiting for it to crumble upon him.

A little flight of arrows fluttered across the sky and dropped among the teams jamming the gate. An ox twisted to stare white-eyed at the feathered wand trembling in its side. The team wedged crosswise in the sallyport.

Cary saw the whacker drop from his wagon and try to force his way through the gate into the fort. He slashed at his face with his Stetson. "Cut that bull loose and get your wagon inside!"

He dismounted to throw off the oxbow. They wrestled the animal out of the team. The wagons lunged on. Remounting, Cary saw that the bulk of Stockwell's line had formed raggedly in a flat crescent. Beyond, a trio of skinners who had abandoned their wagons in the stream were sprinting for the post. A warrior in advance of the others rode alongside and sank a war-axe in a teamster's head.

Through the turmoil of dumped freight and overturned wagons, the final wagon of Cary's string wallowed into the passageway. Above him, he heard the first crashing volley of fire from the walls. He vaulted into his saddle and loped out.

"All right—bring them in!"

Stockwell shouted the word to his teamsters. Snatching up horns and rifles, they sprinted for the fort.

6

The Last Stand

THE PASSAGE STRANGLED WITH THE REEK OF RIFLES,
long rays of sunlight coasting goldenly through the dust
and smoke. Four of the post workers were hauling the
gates to. Cary and three others waited, rifles to shoulder, for the last stragglers to sprawl inside. A hundred
feet out, a shirtless skinner sprawled. A dozen Sioux
rushed over him, mounted warriors streaked with yellow, black and vermilion. An arrow slanted in and lay
in the dust of the tunnel.

The gates shouldered together. A moment later a
thudding force piled against the logs. There was a high
and muted fury from many throats. A salvo of riflefire
rippled from the blockhouse. The thudding finished.
Someone with his mouth against the gate began to
moan.

They retreated, barring the inner gate. The post had
come wildly to life. Wagons and bull-teams surged in
dusty turmoil. Whackers dragging long plains rifles

clambered to the roofs of buildings. The fore-blockhouse rocked with gunfire. A man on the catwalk below the grayed teeth of the wall sprinted low with a keg of black powder in his arms.

In all this hash of confused men and deserted animals, Cary glimpsed one man standing solemnly near the gate with a carbine crooked in his elbow and his hat on the back of his head, soberly inspecting the pageant. Donovan had a smut of powder across his forehead. Sam abandoned his horse in the corral and swung to Donovan.

"Are you in this?"

"That gate won't hold long." Donovan said.

"It won't have to. They won't get past the outer one. Get up there to the blockhouse and take over. I'll send up the Springfields."

The chaos of firing swelled again, smoke eddying from the tall slots of the blockhouses. A low, insistent thunder spoke of a battering ram against the gate. On the wall, ramrods rose and fell.

Silvertooth was fighting to get the teams corralled, his voice complaining in bitter baritone curses. Cary thrust through the log-jam of tall wheels and weathered boxes, sorting among them until he found the arms-wagon. He gathered a crew to open the chests and carry armloads of greasy Springfields to the catwalk. He caught a case under his arm and ran to a building wedged into the southwest corner of the walls. Atop the married men's quarters, four men lay in an acrid fume of smoke, loading, ramming, firing.

Cary sprawled among them. He pressed his cheek to a rifleloop and peered down. The horde of Sioux milling before the gate had swelled. The gate was bowing to the very weight of greasy flesh. In the thickening dusk, two or three hundred warriors fired up at the walls, while others hammered at the gate with cottonwood logs. The main force still lingered behind the wagon-boxes of Stockwell's ruined train, waiting for the rush when the gate went down. Their muskets flashed, flights of arrows soared into the fort; knuckles thudded red war-drums.

Cary nudged the barrel of the Henry into the loophole. A ball smacked close beside it, fanning yellow splinters over the opening. In that dusty turmoil of warriors, he looked for Esconella's white ghost-shirt, the clay-whitened doeskin tunic said to be proof against bullets. But the war chief was back in the trees.

He gouged sixteen .44 balls into the horde of warriors, and sat back to fill the tube. A rifleman jolted off a shot and turned to grope for a shell. He ejected the smoking copper case and slipped a new cartridge home, and then in sober amazement looked at Cary.

"Greased lightnin'?" he said.

The firing fattened, as other Springfields came into action. Wounded warriors dragged themselves away from the walk; a gang of Tetons carried a wounded chief back to the wagons. Horses were down and others pitched wildly through the bitter twilight of black powdersmoke. The attack slowly slackened for lack of impetus.

The firing from the walls subsided. The Indians had given back. Single shots rang through the smoke drifting from the walls. Donovan's voice mounted peremptorily.

"Doctor Merritt! A man's wounded up here."

Somewhere in the gray dusk, the envoy called, "I'm coming, man."

Cary slumped back and could not ease the crabbed grip of tension.

Dusk flooded Young Woman Valley. A rusty green stained the sky above the marbled Bighorns. From the litter of wagons, hissing swarms of arrows arched; rifle fire crusted along the ground and winked out.

Dark came on. The angry legion began to work into bivouacs, warriors from each tribe and village guarding their identity. Fires blinked, glistening bodies slipped back and forth, working up to a dance. Skin rattles shook. Through a fiber of writing bodies, Cary saw something that lay gauntly, pincushioned with arrows— one of the skinners who had not made it to the fort.

He smoked a pipe, glancing from time to time toward the creek. A faint fog of stars misted the sky. At eight o'clock he shoved himself up. He struck the pipe against his hand.

"Four-hour watches," he said. "They won't attack tonight, but they'll be crawling up for the dead and wounded. Let them have them. It may be all they'll want. But if they get too thick, watch out."

He descended from the wall. A cramped little city, the post lay in a silent paralysis. He opened the door of the mess-shack and shouted for the cooks. He had coffee and venison put on for half the crew, and then strode along the wall, calling men down.

In the blockhouse, he found Merritt finishing with the wounded skinner. A red stain drenched the linsey-woolsey of the man's right thigh. "We'll carry him to the powder magazine," Merritt said. "It will do for a field hospital."

Cary went ahead. He sounded the signal on the thick portal. A small stone cell, the magazine was buried to half its depth in the earth. After a moment the door opened an inch and a gun-muzzle gleamed darkly. Then Gaybird cried out and let Sam push the door open.

Dale Merritt crowded through to clutch the doctor. Ignoring her, Merritt directed the litter-bearers inside. "They've pulled off for the night," Cary said.

Dale turned quickly. "But surely they won't attack again? Haven't they had enough?"

"Jericho had walls, too," said Cary. "You ladies can sleep in your rooms tonight, but you'll come back here at four o'clock. Food will be ready in a few minutes."

Daniel Edge walked to the mess with Sam and Gaybird. He wiped his mouth on his sleeve, an over-heavy man with a seawalk. "The Pilgrims never had it harder," he said bitterly.

Sam and Gaybird sat across a long table from each other. A distant surf sounded in Cary's ears, remnant of the firing. Gaybird was soberly occupied with her thoughts.

"Tell me about Crazy Dog," she said finally.

"I'd rather tell you about a girl I know."

"Would I like her?"

"She's a hummingbird in armor. Even a thousand Sioux can't upset her."

Her chin began to tremble then. "You'd better tell me about Crazy Dog," she said.

"The chief's going to walk. Merritt took a bullet out of him."

"And he'll come to Laramie for the parley?"

"He said he'd be there."

"Then there's still some chance . . ."

A rifle exploded in the night—and echoes cascaded through the post. It was silent again. The Pawnee cook brought steaks and coffee. Sam regarded her with a sober smile.

"Will it be worth it, Gaybird? We may never see the time when you can ride out without wondering what's behind the next ridge. Will anything be worth that?"

"I've never seen it any other way," she declared slowly, "and it's always been worth it."

Afterward, with Gaybird in her own room behind the commissary, Cary made a slow tour of the post. It was now past ten. Each roof had its silent watchers. The blockhouses had their sharpshooters who smoked quietly with rifles across their knees. He mounted the wall. In the fore-blockhouse the smoky darkness was restless with low talk and snoring. Shells and burned primers crunched under his boots as he crossed the floor. He kicked a bucket of water, and swore under his breath. The air was choked with tobacco fumes. He put his palms against the wall and peered through a slot.

He thought he saw a wagon moving. He heard Donovan growl,

"They've pulled away half their dead. They may quit when they git 'em all."

"Keep thinking it, if you want. It's as good a prayer as any."

Coy Mullan's voice said testily, "I never seen the Injun yet that liked climbing while he was being shot at."

Cary put his back to the wall, thinking about the wagon. "We can't shoot at a thousand of them at once, if they swarm together."

"What'll they climb on? Ladders?"

"No," Cary said. "Wagons."

The blockhouse was quiet. Someone grunted and shifted his position, and a muleskinner growled, "—Wagons. Yes. That'd be the caper."

Mullan rose from a corner and stood by the trapdoor. He was silent a moment. He said roughly, "I'll go down and have a bait. When you've time, Cary, I want a talk with you."

You want to tell me it was all Stockwell's fault about the rifles, Cary said to himself. You didn't know he was planning it, until it was too late. I know the story.

"When I've got time," he said, "will be when the Sioux have left. Send up a bucket of coffee."

Reliefs came. Carrying their rifles, the men descended the ladder. A last man slouched in beside Cary as he stepped onto the catwalk.

"We did have a date at Fort Graybull, didn't we?" said Donovan. "This is Graybull, now, eh?"

"We did have."

"There's been times you were thirty seconds from a ball in the back. That's happened in the army. Only I fight from the front. Why did you think you could handle me like a greenhorn?"

"One of us," Cary said, "had to handle the other. You'd have been handling me before we reached Fort

Reno. It's a point with you not to be handled by anybody. You must have gone crazy in the army.''

''. . . I bought out after six months. Then—my God!—I ran into you. Was it any business of yours how I drank and worked, so long as I got my chores done?''

''There's only one commodity I can make money out of,'' Sam told him. ''Men. All the trade goods in Wyoming won't do me any good if I can't move my wagons. Some men can pack goods with less loss than others, and now and then a man can pack a wagon, whack bulls and fight Indians too. I don't know why I picked you for one of those. Silvertooth told me I was crazy. I picked you the way I'd pick a horse—with the heart more than the head.''

''What do you like in a work-horse?''

''Something that doesn't fight the bit. You fight the bit because you think discipline is beneath you. Donovan, it isn't beneath anybody! The sergeants you fought with were under discipline to the shavetails. The shavetails answered to the captains, and back in Washington there's a general with poor digestion who's under discipline to every man and woman in the country.''

Donovan peered solemnly into Cary's eyes as though to be sure he was not being joshed. He asked scoffingly, ''Who do *you* answer to?''

''To you. And to all the other men I'm supposed to move through hell without getting the smell of fire on them.''

Donovan shifted his rifle. He looked down suddenly. He muttered, ''Well, that's one way of looking at it . . .'' Solemnly, he went down the ladder.

Cary remained in the blockhouse until three-thirty, sleeping a little. There was the depressing air of an army hospital ward. Most of the men lay on the floor, turning much and sleeping little, their breathing heavy. A teamster startled them all by coming out of a nightmare with a yell and lunging to his feet. Someone threw a dipper of water on him and he sank down, shaken.

Dawn would begin about four-thirty. One hour . . . Cary checked the ammunition, took a last look at the Sioux camp and sensed a throb of movement in it. He left John Silvertooth in charge and went down to rouse all the relief men.

As he descended the ladder, a rifle-shot tore the pre-dawn silence. He stared at the corrals, from which the shot had come. A sentry shouted and there was a bristling of guards along the walls. But in a moment someone called, "Go back to sleep. Owls ought to know better than to roost on walls anyway."

The man sauntered from the rear of a storehouse which backed up to the corral. He halted, leaning against the poles, and ejected a shell from his rifle. Cary moved from the ladder and went along the corral fence until he reached the man. It was Mark Stockwell.

Stockwell slowly thrust the bolt of his rifle forward and they regarded each other in the tingling gray of early dawn. "Won't be long now," said the Montanan. "I wonder how much of my freight will be left?"

"It doesn't seem to worry me," Cary said.

". . . You're nursing your suspicions for all they're worth, aren't you?"

"Found a hole to crawl through?" Cary asked. He saw him clearly—saw the tough, aggressive mind which would wriggle out of any trap. He was a nice balance of greed, lack of squeamishness, and egotism—the kind of far-sighted egotism that sometimes got a man's profile on a coin or a postage stamp, and sometimes got him hanged.

Stockwell said, "Orrum was a damned fool. I warned him against leaving the train, but he was in a hurry to see that French girl of his in Butte. He had a load of old Harper's Ferry's I was buying from him. I dickered for your Springfields once, too; remember? I told him to leave them at the post and my manager would pay him."

Cary did not reply. Stockwell stirred under his regard and demanded testily, "Well, what did you think?"

"You know what I think. I mean to put you in the guardhouse when we get through this. You'll go back to Cheyenne in irons. You can handle your own men better than I can or I'd have locked you up before now. And we need your gun. We need every gun, to match the ones you put in their hands."

Stockwell said, "I'd like to see any ten of you put me in irons."

"You will."

Cary walked away from him. At the rear blockhouse he made his inspection. He located Donovan in the mess hall. He sat down across from him with a mug of coffee. Donovan's eyes nestled in tired, puckered flesh. His face was surly, as a good foot-soldier's should have been.

"I'm going to leave you in charge of the yard," Cary stated. "I want the freight dumped from eight or ten of the wagons and a barricade made out of the boxes. Lay them out to face the gate."

"What makes you think they'll come in that way?"

"Because if they start moving wagons up to the walls, I'll open the gates."

Donovan pressed his fingers against his eyes. "I'm tired. I don't hear things right. You said . . . ?"

"I'll open the gates. Let them in. If they storm us at too many points, we can't stop them. They'll be all over the post, setting fires."

"And how in thunder do you think you're going to stop eight hundred at one spot?"

"With fire power. It's the only way we can hope to. You don't have to kill every man in an army to lick it. If we can pile them up shoulder-deep at the entrance, the others are going to lose heart. Especially if we can make a liar out of Esconella, with his bullet-proof ghost-shirt."

"Let them in!" Donovan muttered, peering darkly down into his coffee cup.

Cary rose from the bench. "Maybe we won't have to. But if we do, I want the wagons ready."

A rifle roared. Another hammered out its horde of echoes; then a crackling of shots from the south wall broke out. Cary shouted to the room, "Get to your posts!"

Outside, a murky light seeped from the sky. Tongues of fire licked through a slot in the blockhouse. A guard bawled, "They're bringing up the wagons! Let's have some of you coffee-swillers up here . . ."

Cary went back to the blockhouse. From the ladder, he looked down to see Donovan impressing teamsters into service. A man shook off his hand. Donovan struck him with the back of his fist and sent him reeling toward the wagons. Cary climbed into the dim reek of powdersmoke.

The dregs of night lay over the fields. Through river mist he discerned the gaunt shapes of freight wagons moving down both sides of the post. One was already against the sallyport. There was no evidence of bull-teams. A dozen Sioux could push a wagon without difficulty, lurking on the off side so that they were protected from rifle fire. Yet the main horde of Ogalalla, Brule and Uncpapa warriors remained among the vestiges of Stockwell's freight.

Rifle fire rippled up and down the walls. The wagons came on, ghostlike in the dawn. Inside the post, a wagon went over with a splintering crash. Cary turned to study the yard. One or two wagons had been unloaded and moved into place about fifty feet from the inner gate of the sallyport. Donovan had now given up unloading them and his workmen were pushing them into place loaded and overturning them with a bull-team.

Cary turned to Silvertooth. "Take over the walls, John. Hold the men as they are until the attack begins. I figure it will be at the main gate. When it comes, take most of the men to the front and pour it into them."

Crusty with fatigue and tension, Silvertooth growled, "You seem damned sure they'll play it your way."

"I aim to make it so attractive they can't pass it up. What's more tempting than an open gate? But we knock them over as they come through."

"And what's more suspicious! Esconella's a fox, not a fool. Sometimes I think you're crazy!"

"This is going to be convincing."

He descended the ladder and slung off to the rear posts to pass the word. Oxen and horses surged anxiously about the corral as he strode by.

He headed for the rear posts, but in the shadows back of the commissary he stumbled over something. He caught himself and looked back. Puzzled, he returned to the man who lay against the log wall. This man's cheek was against the earth. His arms were drawn under him and one leg was pulled up. Cary pulled him onto his back. Coy Mullan looked up at him with filmy blue eyes. His throat had been torn by a bullet and there was a grisly display of cords and muscles.

He hoarded something in his hand—a clutch of buckskin whangs, a handful of fringe torn from the yoke of someone's shirt. Cary regarded him grimly.

. . . Owls ought to know better than to roost on trading post walls, and wagonmasters should know enough not to question their employer's motives. Coy Mullan had learned this too late. . . .

A man of ideas, Donovan had placed crates of hardware in random fashion just within the inner gate. The warriors who rushed through it would not come on a straight line. Their charge would be slowed and blunted. Cary made a hand, helping to overturn the wagons. Between the boxes they threw up a shallow earthworks. A pattern grew: A wide halfwheel of wagon boxes confronting the gate; crates radiating from the hub like stubends of sunken piles. A second, paralleling ring of boxes began thirty feet behind the first; the final firing line.

Crates of shells were split open and scattered for ready loading. Cary was sweating. He came face to face with the question of whether he had forgotten anything

. . . any *pons asinorum* of military strategy which might suddenly backlash on him.

Donovan was manning the boxes with teamsters as fast as the wagons were overturned. Axes made rough loopholes in the bottoms of the boxes. As Cary brought up a crate of shells, Donovan growled, ''I'd like to meet the fella who said Injuns don't besiege.''

''After today, maybe he'll be right. Or it might be that white men won't build forts any more. You'll stay with the second rank. Pick off any who get past us, and move over if we have to pull back.''

He found Daniel Edge. ''Dan, I've a chore for you.''

Edge blinked slowly and pulled a forearm across his forehead. ''I know. I reckon that's what I get for bein' fat.''

''That's what you get for being fat and trustworthy. You won't go soft?''

''God keep me from it. And God help all of us, Sam.''

Edge labored slowly past the commissary toward the powder magazine. Sam saw him pat his shirt pocket, like a man leaving on a scout, who checks to see whether he has his matches.

She came to him then in a little cameo of vision, smiling and sweet, sitting on a wagon tongue as she brushed her blue-black hair. It struck him bitterly that nothing should be so hard as this, nothing so lonely and full of consequences.

And now Silvertooth came to the window of the blockhouse and roared down, ''Something's up! Esconella's ranging up and down the line. Make your play, if you're going to.''

The darkness of the powder-magazine was warm and thick as smoke. Gaybird sat on a pallet against the wall, a bucket of water where she could reach it at her right, a rifle on her lap, the wounded man at her left. There was an odor of sickness and medicines. That, and the monotonous, snoring moans the man made, burdened the darkness.

It was tiring to have the eyes opened, focused on nothing. It was more tiring to squeeze them shut. While she sat there, she worked on knitting she had brought from her wagon. Her needles made a tiny, good-natured prattle. Sound suddenly pricked through the stone walls, like a distant crackling of flames. Gaybird's heart compressed.

There was a scratching sound and light broke dazzlingly in the room. Dale Merritt was on her knees a few feet away, holding a dripping wax match in her fingers.

"I won't sit in the darkness like—like a criminal waiting to be executed!" she cried. "Why did they have to put this man in with us? Why—"

Gaybird said firmly, "Put the match out!" She was not looking at Dale, but at the crates and kegs of shells and powder.

Dale struggled up. "I'll not put it out! If we've got to stay here, I'll know whether it's rats or Indians I hear!"

She faced Gaybird furiously. Gay quietly raised a dipper of water from the bucket and hurled it. The light was extinguished. Dale began to sob.

"Just sit down," Gaybird told her, "and think less of us and more of them out there. That isn't so nice, what they're doing. Much less nice than waiting."

At the same time, she was not so sure. Now that the rifle-fire was a full-throated roaring, she had to cease knitting. Her fingers were unsteady. The wounded man began to mouth a word, over and over. She gave him water.

Then she sat back and thought of Sam. She wished she had done one thing last night: Given him the ring and asked him to put it on her finger. But it had all been too confused for sentiment, and now, perhaps, he might never do it.

Dale was whispering: "But they can't get in, can they?"

"I don't know. I don't think so."

"If they do, what will happen? I mean—what do they do to—to women?"

"Sometimes they make slaves of them. They don't covet us as one might think. They have contempt for white flesh."

The stronghearted lie. What *did* the braves do? And what did the squaws do, drunk on jealousy and cruelty? She was not sure, because men did not tell such things to women.

The door sounded to the signal knock. Quickly she crossed the dark floor to open it. The cold, gray dawn seeped in. Fat Daniel Edge stood there smiling, a short-axe in his hand.

"Ladies," he said heartily, "we thought you might be wanting company. I see you brought your knitting, Gaybird. Sam said to be sure you put heels in his socks this time. You left them off, last time, you remember." Dan's smile grew broader.

He came in, closing the door on the shocking thunder of the rifles. They heard him cross the floor toward the powder kegs. The axe made a single, sharp smack against a keg, and a piece of wood fell to the floor.

Dale said hastily, "You may sit over here by me, if you want, Mr. Edge. There's a pallet."

Dan Edge seemed to yawn. "No, I'll be quite well right here." He made himself comfortable on the split-open top of the powder keg.

Cary took his horse from the line and loped through the wagons, striking Donovan on the back as he passed. He found Tom Kane, the scout, and shouted, "Come along!"

The gate bars were dressed eight-by-eights. The two men lifted them out of the iron hasps. The gate swung slowly outward. Cary mounted again and looked out. He had again the feeling that the dammed-up fury of the wilderness must rush into this gap, forcing it like a hole in a dike. In the gray dawn, he witnessed the pre-attack skirmishing of the Sioux, the little pointless rushes, the rattled weapons and curvetting ponies, which corresponded to a white man's spitting on his palms and settling down to work. He heard their sharp animal yelping.

Esconella, distinctive in his famed white ghost-shirt, a red blanket across his lap as he sat his pony, had discovered the open gate. He sat utterly still.

Between the gate and the wagons lay the body of the murdered teamster. He was naked, and bristled with arrows. Cary said to Kane, "Back away, now, and get to your post. Let the first man through—it had better be me."

He spurred the horse out of the post and crossed the torn, bloody ground before the gate. The silence of the walls ached in his ears. He loped for the corpse of the muleskinner. Reaching it, he swung his pony broadside to the Indians and slid off on the post side. He crouched beside the dead man, not touching him, not looking at him: There was nothing he could do for the dead man, but there might be something the skinner could do for him. Recovering your dead—there was something an Indian could understand.

Then a yell like the scream of a mountain lion came from a bronze throat. A gun cracked. Peering under the barrel of the horse, Cary saw the line begin to melt toward him. Ponies and mounted warriors oozed through gaps in the wagons. Clots of horsemen flowed around the ends. The wilderness had found the hole in the dike.

Cary lunged for the pony. With his hand on the saddle-horn, he felt it quiver. He heard the *pop* of an arrow entering the tough little body. The horse sank down, biting at the feathered shaft in its side. Cary turned to run.

The Springfields began to shout, throwing out dirty-black smoke and shuddering explosions. It seemed, at that moment, that all hell had broken loose.

Behind him, the line was shredding, the faster ponies racing ahead of the others. As he reached the gate, he turned to raise his carbine. A breechclouted warrior carrying a musket and a bullhide shield led the pack. Sam put him on the tip of the Henry and fired. He felt the quivering of earth under the horses' hoofs, and just as he turned into the gate he saw the Sioux throw his hands up and leave the wooden saddle.

Cary ran through the deserted sallyport and entered the post. Crates studded the ground like stumps. He dodged through them to the first line of wagon-boxes. He sprawled behind a box and came into a kneeling position with one foot kinked under him. He raised his gun to steady it against the gray wood of the tail-gate. He was gasping for breath. His hand pulled at the loading lever, inching it down, thrusting it back, until angrily he smacked it home and circled his finger through the trigger-guard.

There was the boom-and-echo of rifles along the catwalk. Riflemen jolted to the kick of the guns. Suddenly a man ran from the blockhouse and came halfway down the steps, to sit down and wait, his rifle trained on the crates.

The flat hammering of pony-hoofs filled the passage. An Indian was shouting soprano invective. The sallyport seemed gagging on its gorge of oncoming Indians and horses.

A naked Sioux with rifle and reins in his left hand and a coup-stick raised in his right lunged out of the passage. The teamster on the steps got his shot in an instant ahead of the others: The Sioux dropped the rifle. The other balls struck him simultaneously, changing the look of his face and breast. His pony swerved and kicked out at a crate. The next horse ran broadside into him. A rifleman knocked its rider onto the ground.

It was suddenly as if a dam had broken. Cary felt his body know itself. He was in the path of a flood. It boiled with a flotsam of horsehide, of copper skin streaked blue and red and green. Lances, bows and rifles tossed and thrummed and roared.

He found himself firing. A hot shell stung his cheek.

A hand which did not seem to be his slapped the loading lever down and up. He was firing into the howling vortex of ponies and riders. The quadrangle was choking on them. Scores . . . hundreds . . . you could not fail to hit.

A splatter of color broke off and bubbled through the boxes, getting behind his wagon: A half-dozen Sioux had broken the first line of defense. They swung and charged back, and one of them fired a musket and a man was shouting, "My arm, my arm!"

Bullwhackers were sprawling everywhere and their shots were a stuttering clap of thunder. There was not an Indian on his pony an instant after the six broke through. Someone flopped onto a scrambling brave and a skinning knife fell.

Cary's eyes lingered on a gray stone structure beyond all this, tucked in behind a building at the rear . . . the powder magazine. I hope she can't hear. I don't want her to have it to remember. And she must remember, she must be able to look back on this day. It will not all end for her before the sun climbs the wall.

He looked back. Another dozen Indians could not be packed into that shouting square. Crates were overturned and spilled. Blankets, white crockery and jugs of vinegar tangled the ponies' hoofs. Horses lay on their backs, screaming and kicking at the air. A bitter smoke wound through the buildings. The fort was a travail of the dying.

The cauldron was filled. The pressure in back was greater than the restraint of the wagon boxes and rifles, and in an instant it would boil over on the riflemen.

Cary lurched up, shouting, "Back up! Keep firing!"

They gave back stubbornly. Some of Donovan's men retreated to the porch of the commissary. A tall Ogalalla with an eagle-bone through his top-knot and a knife in his teeth rushed a teamster. A double-bitted axe met him. The Indian went down in a full run.

Hunched behind the box, Cary reloaded the Henry.

He raised it again and dully chose a target. Then something in the crowd of warriors screamed for his attention.

There he is! Cary yelled. Clay-whitened, its stippling of blue porcupine quills just visible, Esconella's ghost-shirt was struggling forward. A lance flashed, fluttering a fresh scalp as the point came down into the body of a teamster caught in the muck of Indians.

Then the shirt again came ahead, twisting through the mob, seeming truly to be magic. Rising slowly, Cary went to meet it.

Esconella guided his horse with his knees. He held the lance high, blood dripping from the point. Arrogance burned in his face. This is his day, Cary thought; his hour. The first war chief to overpower a fort! Across his face yellow-and-black bars shone greasily. His eyes found Cary standing beside the wagon-box. The moccasined heels struck the pony's ribs. He leaned forward, his arm carrying the lance back.

Cary raised the carbine and pulled the trigger.

The hammer fell without a sound. He looked dumbly at the gun. Empty . . . He swore and dropped it, reaching blindly for his Colt, but Esconella was over him, driving the lance in. He felt the point tug at his armpit and go through his shirt. Something sleek and sharp chattered across his ribs. His hands closed on the shaft of the lance. He hauled back and the Sioux released it. The lance fell. Esconella reached for his revolver—Bill Orrum's Colt—but Cary was lunging in to seize the Indian's leg and drag him out of the saddle. The roman-nosed warrior was on top of him as they went down.

They were on the ground. Cary's hand closed on the rancid mat of hair. He held the lean head down and rolled over to pin the twisting body with his own. Gory fingers closed on his throat. His free hand groped at his hip, searching. Now it closed on a smooth, corrugated cylinder of bone and he pulled his case-knife free. He let Esconella see the knife. He felt the fingers leave his throat, and drove quickly. The knife struck Esconella's collar bone; it slanted off into his throat. Sam struck again, and a third time.

He stood up and dragged the chief's body behind the wagon. He cut the bloody shirt from it and found a discarded rifle to hang it on. Jamming the gun between the spokes of a wheel, he let the shirt dangle where the Sioux could see it.

Up on the catwalk there was a wild yelling. The old, primitive story was still good business, Cary reckoned: Chief slaying chief.

A brave discerned the shirt and rode forward to recover it. Bullets began to hit him; he kept coming, but within reach of it a final ball slugged him aside. He was down in the roil of hoofs and dust.

Heated to smoking, the Springfields still rammed their machine-made bullets out; the queer bolts lifted and the copper shells slid home, and chunks of fifty-caliber lead roared out in a fog of brackish smoke.

It was coming home to the Sioux: These were fifty men with the fire power of two hundred. Esconella had lied to them. There was no magic in his deerskin tunic. There was no wisdom in his strategy.

Cary saw the beginning of the pressing-back. With a full magazine, he stepped into the interval between the rings of wagon-boxes and commenced firing. Sweat trickled saltily onto his lips. This was a cowpen slaughter. They were not fighting: They were running, riding, crawling—back to the sallyport. There they ran into the glut of braves still dreaming of scalps and high deeds.

Cary brought the rifle up again and frowned across the sights.

Indians did not comprehend surrender, but they understood retreat. You retreated when the hearts of your gods turned bad. You retreated when you had to climb the backs of your own butchered companions to get at the enemy. Nearest the gate, the bucks fought back into the passage. Among the wagon-boxes, marooned warriors battled with clubbed rifles and broken lances. It was a massacre from mythology.

Cary had had enough. He raised his arm. *"Hold your fire!"*

But no one heard him. The rifles continued to roar. Men continued to fight. Men continued to die.

The eternal sun came up, as if reluctantly, to peer through the smoke and dust. A torpid reaction had rotted the life of the post after the retreat. Across Young Woman Creek, a mauled army of Sioux lurked among the trees, waiting for nightfall, when they could recover their dead. If the white man comprehended the etiquette of warfare, he would place the dead and wounded on the ground before the post.

Gray with powder-grime, Cary saw to the caring-for of the wounded and tolled off a dozen men to carry the dead outside. As the wounded were cared for, they were laid beside the dead.

He remembered Coy Mullan. Now that significance came back to such small things as a single murdered wagonmaster, he remembered Mullan. . . .

He had seen Mark Stockwell helping to carry a wounded whacker into the dispensary, but he had not seen him since.

Cary went past the commissary and turned into the alley between the long building and a storehouse. A cold night gloom clung close to the ground. He saw Mullan's body. Pressed against the unbarked log of the commissary was another figure. He drew his Colt. The man held Mullan's right hand in both of his, but he dropped it quickly and rose to his feet.

They were face to face, fifteen feet apart. Stockwell was a gray, hunched figure without a hat. He made a hopeless gesture.

"Done for Coy, they did," he said. "Shot in the throat."

"Yes, before the fight started," Cary said. "I saw

the fringe in his hand. You should have come back for it before his fingers froze.''

Stockwell moved away from the wall. A dark gleam of metal showed the upward movement of his hand.

In the alley there was one great throb of sound, a single, stunning heartbeat. Then sound flowed out both ends of it and Cary was alone with a man who lounged woodenly against the wall, and dropped his gun, and sank to his knees.

Darkness came down Young Woman Creek and shapes moved on the meadow. Pickets observed them from the walls. In the dispensary, someone lighted a lamp. Doctor Merritt had been asleep with his head on the table. He looked up to see his wife placing the lamp before him. She appeared very thin and pinched, but she had brushed her hair and changed her gown. She came across the scrubbed, wet floor.

''Asa, you must come to bed. You're exhausted.''

He shook his head. ''Dead.''

''We have a nice room next to Mr. Edge's. I have some marvelous beef broth for you—and real coffee!''

Merritt leaned forward; he looked as though he were falling out of the chair. But he put his palms on his knees and slowly levered himself onto his feet. ''All I want is sleep. All I'll ever want. I've been riding or fighting or doing surgery for—how long? Two days. That's a long time, for a little Washington politician.''

She held his arm and smiled at him, more in coaxing than in persuasion. ''And still, we had good times in Washington, didn't we?'' she said. ''And we shall have again. It's all very well to be patriotic, but we've earned something better than Wyoming. We're going home, Asa!''

He was silent, looking about the cramped little chamber. Behind this minute surgery was the infirmary; he would be back here a dozen times tonight. Yet there was a species of comfort in the thought. These men, when they summoned him, were a continent removed from dissimulation. When they said, *I need you,* they meant it.

"I won't go back to Washington," he said. "I'll send my report from Fort Russell."

Dale's hands dropped away. She looked at him like a child meeting punishment. "You'll go back to your practice?"

"I am thinking," Merritt said, "of contracting to the army. There are forts in this country without a single surgeon."

Men were coming across the ground from the commissary. Someone spoke drunkenly and dragged his feet.

Dale's lips parted. Her face grew lax and her hands clenched.

Merritt stood up, smiling. "If it's prestige you want, my dear, I'll be the most important man on the post. I'll wear a uniform. You'll be Mrs. Doctor Merritt, and no officer's lady would dare give a tea without inviting you."

Two men ascended the steps and crossed the porch with a third man halfcarried between them. It was Tom Kane, the scout. Kane's face had been mauled. All three of these men gave off vapors of whiskey.

"A little disagreement," said one of the teamsters. He helped seat Kane on the table. "This fella was recruiting a company to mine gold. He tried to get Donovan to make a hand, and Donovan whipped him. He promised the same to any other man who tried to leave before the end of the season. Funny thing because Donovan was only drinking beer."

"Not so funny," the doctor murmured. . . .

After he had pulled together a cut in the man's eyebrow and mended his lip, he let him go. They heard the trio leave; then the doctor backed down the flame of the lamp, left it on the table and took his wife's arm. She did not move. Merritt regarded her and said gently,

"Of course I wouldn't make you stay. If you don't happen to like this country, nothing can make you."

Something about her at that instant—some softness of indecision—made him think of the first year of their marriage. Dependency in a woman was a fine thing.

"Do you want me to go back?" she asked him.

Merritt held her hands, slowly shaking his head. "I think you know what I want you to do."

Dale came against him and began to weep.

It was late when Gaybird found Sam in the armory.

Now he was fitting the Springfields into wall racks, except for a few chests stored against the wall. The stocks had been rubbed with linseed oil and the browned steel had a moist lustre.

"I think you're in love with them," she said.

Cary padlocked the retainer and dropped the key in his pocket. "I brought them up here to sell," he said, "but I'll hang onto them now until the army comes back. That may not be long."

She watched him move cases of ammunition about. He frowned over the arrangement. "Maybe those ought to go into the powder magazine."

"I'm sure I wouldn't know," she said.

Cary saw, without appearing to, that she wore the candy-striped gown she had worn in Cheyenne. It gave her the silhouette of a hand-bell, a slender stem above, a generous flair from the waist, her slippers just visible. She wore a narrow blue sash and a velvet wrist band, and he detected a richer scent than the decorous rose-water fragrance he associated with her. An out-and-out French perfume.

He set one case atop another. "I was worried that there might be rats down there this morning."

"No," she said.

He inspected a gun crate, saying gruffly, "These will have to be nailed down against the dust." Her slippers were silent on the floor, but her dress and petticoats rustled tartly, and just as she reached the door Sam said, "You've put your hair up."

She turned. Her chin was up as well as her hair. "Braids are for girls," she said.

Sam went to her. "And is there anything wrong with girls?"

"Some people seem to think so."

He reached up and found the bone hairpins which made a coronet of her rich, dark braids. He drew them out and let the braids fall forward over her shoulders. He ran his hands down them. "That's it! You looked like a business partner that way. . . . I almost forgot to tell you about the upstairs room your father had," he said.

"I suppose there are guns stored in it, too?" A smile brushed her lips.

"Guns? There's a new goosefeather mattress on the bed and a crockery bowl and pitcher. I put down some Indian rugs last spring."

"Well, that's nice," she said. "For you?"

"For us," Sam said.

Gaybird bit her lip. Sam picked her up, the silken, rustling froth of her skirts billowing about them. She was pulling something from the bosom of her dress, reproving him: "Sam! This is indecent.—There!" She put the ring in his hand.

Cary laced the ring carefully over her finger. "Didn't I do this once before?"

"But you didn't finish the ceremony. You didn't kiss me."

He kissed her, swaying slightly, their eyes closed. She took a deep, trembling breath when his face moved away. Sam reached for the wall-lamp without taking his eyes from her, and holding it by the ring he carried her into the dark vestibule.

STAGECOACH WEST!

1

CALLAHAN STOOD BEFORE THE RAILROAD SHACK WITH one foot on a crate, slowly smoking a cigar while he watched a dispatcher ramrod the last of a gang of workmen onto a flatcar. The alkali-crusted work-engine, smelling of heated iron and leaking steam and rusty water, bleated once.

The dispatcher stood with his fists on his hips, disciplining the men with his eyes. "Don't look like you were going to a wake," he said. "What happened last night ain't going to happen again. Those Indian hounds won't get the chance. They'll be a cavalry detail waiting at end-of-track this morning."

The train whistled again, the dispatcher waved and the short line of cars loaded with men and materials pulled off into the lavender sagebrush hills. In the cool distance of early morning Callahan saw the vague backbone of the Rockies. Striding back to his office, the dispatcher saw Craig Callahan. He frowned. "I suppose it's a job?"

"Union Pacific man said you were laying track into the mountains," Callahan said.

"We are, but we ain't hiring." He walked past the crate, but Callahan pointed at a rusting pyramid of rails. "Are those regulation?"

". . . They're lighter than regulation," the foreman said. "Why?"

"They looked lighter," Callahan shrugged. "Reckon they'll stand up to mountain travel?"

The railroad man examined the large, dark-haired man in the spotted calico shirt and brown trousers. He seemed to look for irony in the bluff features. Callahan's eyes looked back at him with sober interest, gray eyes with a graining of lines at the outer corners. He looked rough and self-reliant, but he seemed respectful.

"Yes," the dispatcher said, with iron patience. "I think they will hold up or the company wouldn't be using them."

"It's Far-Western, isn't it?"

The man nodded. "Hoagland and Lamerick. What's your name, mister?"

"Callahan. I've worked on southern lines." He smiled and extended his hand. "You're—?"

"Duff," the foreman said, unwillingly. "Well, Callahan, there's nothing for you. We're going slowly. Coloradoans aren't as free with their money as you might have heard, so the company's selling bonds as it goes."

"If I could talk to Superintendent Braga," Callahan said. "I worked with him and Mr. Hoagland on a job in Texas."

"Braga's at Reserve. That's the town we're building to. General offices are there."

Smiling, Callahan straightened. "Excuse all the questions. I just got into Bitter Creek last night. I'd like to get located. Mr. Hoagland would be at Reserve, too, I expect?''

"He happens to be in town. We've got an office here, too. I wouldn't bother him, Callahan. If I were you, I wouldn't bother me any more, either. There's no work for you, but there's plenty for me. Good morning.''

"Good morning,'' Callahan said. "Oh, if you see Braga, tell him I'll be looking him up. And say that he couldn't whip me again, not with me sober. But he'll have his chance.''

There was a gap of silence, and then Duff spoke sharply, but Callahan was crossing the Union Pacific tracks, from which the narrow-gage branch swerved at this point, and he moved northward into the village.

Callahan moved along beneath grayed wooden awnings. Trees had been set out when the U.P. came through ten years before, but they were still scarcely higher than the buildings. This Western Colorado plain was high, and the soil was cold and reluctant. Bitter Creek was a small but prosperous cowtown with a dowry of freighting to Reserve, where miners outfitted for the mountains.

Callahan was staying at the Territorial House, where, he had learned, Marsh Hoagland had his local office. He walked toward the hotel through a stirring of early-morning activity. A shopkeeper, vigorously sweeping boardwalk, gave him a curious stare. A turnout rattled from a livery barn into the street and from a freight corral came a hard volley of hoofbeats and a teamster's shout. Callahan waited for a wagon-and-trailer outfit to rumble by, and crossed to the yellow-fronted hotel, tall and narrow as a door.

He told the desk clerk, "I'm looking for Far-Western.''

"Two-oh-eight,'' the man said. "They don't open till eight, you know.''

"Mr. Hoagland rooms there?''

"When he's in town. But don't—''

"I wouldn't think of it," Callahan agreed.

He breakfasted in the dining room on fried potatoes, steak and coffee. An apple pie in a cheesecloth case caught his eye and he finished on it. It was now seven. He had two men to see. One was Hoagland. The other operated a stage line from Bitter Creek to Reserve: A man named Gentry. It being immaterial which he saw first, Callahan decided to see whether stage men rose earlier than railroad men.

When he went out again, the town had awakened by a few more degrees. Through brisk sidewalk traffic he walked south to the edge of town. There was a large corral here and a small adobe building with a porte-cochere at the side. Just beyond were the steel streaks of the U.P. He entered the front door, but the waiting room and small post-office were empty. Callahan rapped on the counter.

A back door opened and a large, unshaven man in trousers, underwear and no shirt looked out at him. He was thumbing a suspender strap over his shoulder. "Wish for something?" he asked.

"I'm looking for Roy Gentry. If I'm early—"

"Come on back," the man said. "I'm Gentry. Will you have a bait of breakfast?"

"I'd admire some coffee," Callahan said easily.

It was a middle-aged, futile-looking room, Callahan thought. In the corners, a bachelor's broom had seen, heard and disclosed no evil. The rug resembled a very old toupee; an iron cookstove beside the sink was crusted with grease and rust. The bed had not been made, and probably would not be. An old mahogany commode beside an outer door bulged with boots and clothing.

Gentry pulled a skillet from the oven. "I could throw in some more side-pork as easy as not."

A large man, the back of his shoulders was densely haired. Callahan looked quickly for the key to him, and decided it was casualness: Don't hurry a man like Gentry, or he would turn mulish. His hair was worn far down his neck, though he was nearly bald, and his arms were massive. He commenced amputating fat rashers of bacon, and Callahan said, "Thanks, I've eaten."

"Staying at a hotel?"

"The Territorial."

"Used to stay there myself, until I got to runnin' into railroad men every day. Maybe I'm choosy. I started bachin'."

Callahan left his hat on a chair and raised the lid of a blue enamel coffee pot. It was deep with ancient grounds. He started to throw them out, but Gentry said, "Whoop, whoops!" and took the pot from him. "That's the mother," he explained. He added six tablespoons of coarsely-ground coffee and handed it back, smiling. "That's the mother. Orphan coffee ain't worth swillin'."

Callahan chuckled; adding water, he placed the pot on the stove. "This is a friendly town," he observed. "A visitor gets asked to breakfast before you know whether he wants to buy a ticket or sell you a wooden nutmeg."

"Food's cheap," Gentry said easily.

While the room filled with the woody smoke of bacon, the stage man set a small table of splintery deal. Suddenly the room began to tremble. A low growl of thunder seemed to rise from the floor. Gentry strode to the window and yanked out a stick which had supported a pane of the double-hung window. It crashed down but continued to rattle.

"Gol-dang brimstone-burning junkheaps!" he said angrily.

He stood there in snaffled fury until the eastbound passenger train roared past the window. A fine sift of dust shook from the muslin ceiling. Five red passenger cars whipped past the window. Then there were only dust and smoke and a few sparks whirling down.

"There's a well-ballasted road," breathed Callahan,

the spell leaving him. "In another year you'll be able to shave in here and not cut yourself."

"Another year of this," said Roy Gentry, "and I'll be doing my damndest to cut my throat."

He set the table and poured mugs of coffee. "Too strong for you?"

"I only drink for the effect," Callahan said. He stirred sandy gray sugar into the coffee and watched Gentry begin to eat. "Don't think much of railroads, do you?"

"Callahan," Gentry said, "I used to think there was nothing meaner ner dirtier than a drunken Piute Injun. Shows you how wrong a man can be," he said.

"And now you're right on the point of having a railroad to compete with. Going to lick them?"

"I count on the horse-sense of the good people of Colorado Territory to keep me in business," Gentry declared. "Who'd pay money to have cinders blowed in his eyes, sparks in his hair, and be cremated in live steam every time the damned thing jumps the tracks, when he could ride a stage?"

"Spoken like a staging man," said Callahan. "Will you tell me something else? Why do you let them build the road, when you've got a charter that guarantees you exclusive franchise in this area?"

Gentry drank coffee, investigated with his tongue the hiding places of food about his gums, and asked thoughtfully, "How'd you know about that?"

"I spent a month at Reserve finding out things from the County Recorder. You see, I'm thinking of buying a piece of your stage company." Callahan smiled into the frosty gray eyes.

Gentry wiped his mouth on his cuff. "Now *you* tell *me* something. Why is everybody in Bitter Creek in such a hellsweat to invest in a line that's about to be drove to the wall?"

"I didn't know they were."

"You didn't know about this young widow-woman? Winans, I think she calls herself?"

"No. My money's from a little coup in mining. I hate money to gather dust. I've been over your road a dozen times as a passenger this last month. Some of the fords ought to be bridged, but I'd say it was in pretty fair shape. Winans," Callahan reflected. "Where's she from?"

"The Coast. Her late husband was with Birch lines. Fine man, Birch."

"How old is she?" Callahan blew on his coffee.

"Your age, a little younger. Damned sight prettier. I'm taking her to Reserve today on a tour of inspection."

Callahan pointed a finger. "Look out, Roy! She sounds more like the widow of a railroad man, to me. You wouldn't like to have Marsh Hoagland for a partner, would you? A fifty-one per cent partner to vote the line into retirement? You've got them over a barrel if you ever exercise that franchise. They know it. Look out for her."

"I can tell right now you don't know Mrs. Winans. She's innocent as a baby. She was brought up in staging. She wants to stay with it."

"Have you given her a commitment?" Callahan locked his shouting anxiety behind a drawl. It was a guess—that Mrs. Winans was fronting for a railroad a-tremble to legalize its position. But it was a good guess. Hoagland could be crude and direct, but he also knew the bait to use for a trap.

"She's made me an offer," said Gentry easily. "A good price, but she wants control. And I ain't so green as to make a hoss-breaker out of myself."

What Callahan had in mind involved control, also. But he did not mention it. He finished his coffee and rose. "Would you have room for another passenger on that stage today?"

"Sho'."

Callahan said, "Then I'll be here at nine. I'm talking cash, Gentry. I'm no fly-by-night business man. I'm dead serious."

Gentry pumped water into a tea-kettle. "And I'm serious about not selling over forty-nine per cent, young fella. Glad to have you along, though. Don't try to beat my time with Kitty Winans, either."

He chuckled. He probably thought he was joking, Callahan reflected.

Walking back to the Territorial House, Callahan was aware of a feeling of disappointment. He had contrived carefully how he would act once he came out into the open. He had not been more painstaking when he laid out the contours of the ill-fated road Hoagland had built in East Texas. First the partnership with Gentry, for ammunition—the franchise. Then the campaign against Marsh Hoagland.

But Gentry was a tough and prideful man. He must know he was whipped in a lone fight against Far-Western. He could denounce railroads and send his prayers up to the staging gods. Yet, when he faced it, he must know he would not last a month after traffic began to move into Reserve by rail.

And still he could be independent as a cavalry corporal about selling! He would stand in his undershirt and tell a man with money to invest how it was going to be. And it could not be that way, because the only need Craig Callahan had for a stage line was the control of a clause in its charter:

". . . *And that furthermore the operator, his heirs and assigns, shall for a period of fifteen years have full and exclusive right to carry passenger traffic within the legal bounds of San Jose County, as established on Map Number 393 Page—*"

That meant that Far-Western was off-limits by a matter of nine years in attempting to tap the heavy freight and passenger traffic from Reserve, head of navigation below the mountain mines.

It meant specifically that a man could stop construction on the line, and, for once, Hoagland would take the beating.

In his hotel room, Callahan crowded his belongings

into a small carpeted trunk. He loosened his belt; drawing his belly in, he moved up the money belt he wore next to his skin. It was heavy and sweat-inducing. He adjusted his shirt and tightened the belt again. He put on a coat.

Suddenly he was eager for the encounter with Marsh Hoagland. He wanted to see Hoagland's face as he gave him the news—at least half-true—that he had gone into partnership with Roy Gentry. It was entirely possible that the threat would bring Hoagland to time as quickly as the fact.

He trod the carpetless hall to the lobby and turned up the stairs. Hoagland's room was above. As he turned from the upper landing into a yellow-papered hall he saw the door of Room 208 open. A young woman came out. She was a brunette and extremely neat and pretty. Where Callahan loomed with one hand on the spindled rail, it was gloomy. The girl approached him with a handbag hanging from her left wrist. Her heels rang crisply in the hall. She wore a long, lightly-hooped skirt with a snug bodice. Her waist was small and supple. The gray silk gleamed like metal; it sounded to Callahan like the rustle of paper money. A row of buttons down the front of her bodice winked at him, and the long skirt flowed down from her hips with a gay sideward lilt.

For the instant he was dull as a wooden Indian. It came too suddenly: The girl slipping from Hoagland's room at breakfast time. The heart-catching prettiness of her.

Then, in sudden awareness of him, she started and made a little sound. She touched him briefly with dark-eyed horror. Her step lagged, and in the next moment she tripped over a break in the flooring. He heard her gasp as he reached to catch her by the waist. He experienced a soft and fragrant collision, but an instant later she was pulling away. He knew one thing now: Her waist was not boned to such slenderness.

Callahan said, "Easy there, Mrs. Winans!"

She touched the wall with her fingers. "Do we—know each other, sir?"

Callahan removed his hat. "I'm Craig Callahan. You were described to me."

"By whom?" She tried to smile; her lip trembled.

"By a mutual friend."

"Our mutual friend failed to describe you, Mr. Callahan."

"I'm in transportation."

She was utterly off-balance, and he boldly inspected her. Her hair, uncovered by a bonnet, had been encouraged to glistening darkness by a brush; her eyes were a clear russet-brown. He perceived that there was not a straight line in her body. She was small and deep-bosomed. She was the cleanest-smelling human being he had ever stood close to.

All at once she moved to pass him, raising her skirt with one hand. "Good morning, Mr. Callahan. You have the wrong Mrs. Winans."

He stood aside, watching the whispering gray silk float down the stairs. "And you, Mrs. Winans, have the wrong friends," he said gravely.

Again the door of Two-oh-eight opened, and a large man in tan trousers and a brown corduroy coat placed one foot in the hall and glanced toward the stairs. It was Hoagland—cigar, fist-like chin, displeased eyes. No changes there. Callahan leaned against the rail and let recognition come slowly. Finally he saw Hoagland's big chest deflate with an expulsion of held breath.

"Well, well, Craig," he said. "Duff was right. I thought he must have misunderstood."

"Lots of people do," Callahan said, moving toward him.

Hoagland let him come to within ten feet. He said, "It may not show, but I'm wearing a gun."

"I'm not, so relax. That doesn't mean I'm helpless."

Marsh Hoagland smiled. "Braga said you were."

"Ask him again one of these days."

"Did you come out here just to lick Tom Braga?"

"No. To lick you."

Big and lounging and suspicious, Hoagland watched him stop two feet away. Then he stirred. "Come in."

Sitting by a window, Craig Callahan took the whiskey the railroad man offered. "Hear you've got a pardner."

"Lamerick? Banking man from Denver. He's a bearcat for finance. What do you want?"

"An introduction to your friend, first off."

"Lamerick?"

"If that was Lamerick who just left. The brunette with the deep lower lip."

Hoagland's eyes went away. "I don't get you."

"Mrs. Winans."

"You mean the woman next door. Yes, I heard her go out."

"Marshal, Marshal!" Craig grinned.

Hoagland sat down, but when he crossed his legs he was no longer holding his glass, but a pepper-pot derringer. The five barrels, like a dismal and precocious clover-leaf, stared at Callahan. "This town's no different from any other," he said. "A woman's no better than her reputation. Help me keep hers clean." The gun went back to an inside coat pocket, but his eyes stayed with Callahan, bitter as smoke.

"Your love life," Callahan said, "is your own business, so long as it doesn't interfere with my business life."

He let it lie there. Hoagland did not pick it up. He looked genuinely puzzled.

"Forget about my love life," he stated finally. "What's this about your licking me?"

"It will be that," Callahan said, "or a deal with you."

Color flashed through Hoagland's hard features. "It'll be neither, and you're going out of here on your hippockets if you can't talk plain!"

He thumped his glass down. Callahan did not heat.

"Building another railroad like the Texas and Arkansas, Marsh?" he smiled.

"How I build this road is no concern of your," Hoagland said. "Duff said you were crabbing about lightweight rails. Get it through your skull, Callahan, that having been assistant engineer on the T. & A. doesn't make you my special counselor on this job.''

"I'm going to be a little better than that. I'm going to be chief engineer.''

Hoagland made a wry bass oath, and shaking his head, he poured whiskey into his glass.

Callahan leaned forward to rest his elbows on his knees. "And when I finish this one, I'm taking the crew back and put that Texas junkyard on an operating basis.''

Hoagland said drily, "Get out of here.''

"It isn't that I like working for you, mister,'' Callahan said. "It's that I like being able to go where I want to. There's just one state in the Union where I can't go: Texas. They passed a resolution about us at Austin last winter. Nobody who worked on that line, except laborers, can set foot in the state of Texas again. How do you like that, Marsh? How do you like your name written in a big book that you're the worst builder of railroads that ever came down the pike?''

Hoagland said, "They got their railroad. If they wanted to be niggardly about buying bonds, we had to build the best we could.''

"Strap-iron rails and four-by-four ties! They bought better than that. You got your subsidies and bonuses and your cut of the bonds. You let them take one train over it, and then you drifted before it could fall apart.''

"You got yours, too,'' Hoagland snapped. "You got five thousand on top of your salary. Give it back if it's shaming you.''

"I saved it for a purpose. I could give it back to the bondholders, but that wouldn't help them much. I'm putting it to better use. I've bought into a stage line.''

Hoagland nodded slowly. "Just as well you can't go back to Texas. They lock up lunatics down there.''

Callahan, setting the whiskey on the sill, rose. "What do they do to franchise-jumpers?'' He walked past the railroad man, who turned after a moment. Callahan was at the door.

"Gentry won't make trouble," Hoagland said quietly, "and you'd damned well better not. You hear what I say?"

He was on his feet, his long arms hanging, veins corded in his hands. In his face burned the same florid fury he had worn the night they split up in Wichita Falls. A controlled man, he kept his temper on short leash. But when he cut the leash off, he was brutal and blind as a hurt grizzly. Looking at him, Callahan thought: If Braga hadn't been there that night, I'd be dead! If the work boss had not been in the railroad shack when Craig came hunting trouble, drunk on fury and liquor, Hoagland would have shot him. Callahan remembered how Braga had thrust Hoagland away from his racked rifle and taken the younger man for himself.

And now he said, "You aren't dealing with an old stage man, Marsh. You're dealing with me. I've got the franchise. Now I'll get a lawyer. If you build another mile of track on this road, it will be standard, and I'll go along to see that you bridge the gullies instead of swimming them."

He started to turn, one hand on the knob, one in his pocket, but suddenly swung back. Hoagland's hand was inside his coat. His face was a mottled red-gray. Craig Callahan's hand came from his pocket. A nickeled house-gun gleamed in it.

"Turn around, Marsh," he said. "I meant I was *practically* unarmed. This is only a .32. I've heard it takes a whole hatful of slugs to kill a man. Shall we see?"

Hoagland slowly drew his hand from his coat. He turned to the window. He glanced up at the ceiling, his shoulders taut. In a moment he spoke. "I've heard a .45 slug will knock a man flat on his back. Next time we'll see about that."

"Next time," Callahan said, "I'll be wearing a gun where you can see it. I don't think you'll throw down on me then."

A few minutes later, in his own room, Callahan had a moment he was overdue for.

He had taken a holstered Army revolver from his bag and tossed the gun on the bed while he latched the heavy buckle of the belt. The gun pressed a shallow matrix into the blanket, its brass shining, the ruts of the bone handle dark with use. In the field, it had been as familiar to him as his transit. Railroads seemed to invade by choice the passes sacred to Indians. They bridged the streams where they fished or berried. He remembered the dispatcher's invocation that morning, and knew this construction job was no different from any other: It would go forward with due attention to security.

But it was the first time he had had anything but Indians in mind when he buckled on the gun. From this moment, Callahan knew he could not walk down the street or enter a saloon without a gun at his fingertips. He held the Colt on his palm. I've got five thousand dollars, he reflected. I don't have to do this. I could buy a piece of mining property. I could homestead. But I could never railroad again; I've been blackballed from the trade. And I couldn't set foot in Texas. Not that I need to; but telling a man he can't isn't the way to keep him from wanting to.

All these things he had chewed on before he ever set out to track down Marsh Hoagland. They had never seemed so pointed as now, when he tipped the revolver down and slipped it into the basket-woven holster. Let's go, the gesture said.

Until stage-time, he did some purchasing of things scarce in Reserve. At five minutes to nine, he carried his trunk to the stage office. Passengers sat in the sallow spring sunlight before the station. Mrs. Winans was not among them. Under the porte-cochère, Roy Gentry was polishing an oil painting on the olive-green coach panel. He was dressed in a black suit too small for him. He had shaved, cutting his deep sideburns to scimitar-sharpness.

He put Callahan's trunk in the rear boot and consulted a pocket watch. "Mrs. Winans had best shake her pretty limb. Look here,'' he said. Callahan went around to the rear of the Concord coach with him. They inspected a splintered hole above the leather flap of the boot. "Arrowhead?'' he asked.

Gentry nodded. "Coming in last night. Bill Fox says they've been yippin' on the ridges like coyotes for two weeks. Utes; we call 'em Pie-utes over here. It don't make them any tamer. Not when they're abuildin' railroads through their huntin' grounds.'' He shrugged. "This was just a postcard, I expect. 'Havin' fine time. Wisht you were dead.' ''

"Why don't you demand an escort? The railroad draws guards.''

"I sent down for escort last night. Not the first time. Captain Elmo Stanger's quartered at Reserve with a few volunteer troopers. I told him to by-God be at Cross Hollows station this afternoon or he'd get a rump-full of stagecoaches! Don't figger he'll be there, though,'' he added.

In a few minutes a boy came from a hotel with Kathleen Winans' bags. Bill Fox, the driver, appeared, an old man dressed in smoked buckskin pants and shirt, looking like an ancient buffalo-hunter. He carried a copper bugle slung over his shoulder and a knife protruded from his boot. He mounted to the box and the expressman began passing up parcels, and finally the iron-bound express box.

Gentry moved among the passengers. "You gentlemen are armed? Don't want to frighten anybody, but please have your sidearms handy.''

Into the yard hurried a small, slender person in gray silk, whose black velvet bonnet, clinging to the back of her head, danced as she hurried toward the coach. She gave the stage man a pert, sparkling glance.

"I'm always the last,'' she confessed. "Forgive me?''

Callahan complacently waited for her denunciation. Gentry said with gruff good-nature, "We generally leave by the clock, ma'am, not by dead reckoning. Saved you Number One, Kitty, by Mr. Callahan. You two can argue.''

She saw Callahan. Her mouth drew in strained surprise. ". . . That's—Thank you. I don't think—"

"Thought you'd met, by now. Mrs. Winans, Mr. Callahan."

He urged her into the coach with a big, scarred hand. The door slammed behind Craig. The coach was half-full, the jumper seats unoccupied. In rigid silence, he and the girl sat while Gentry handed the lines up to Bill Fox and himself mounted to the left of the box. Fox's horn crowed. The coach sagged back on its bullhide springs and lurched forward. A moment later they banged across the Union Pacific lines and hit out through the gray morning sage.

The girl sat by the window, very young, very pretty, very nervous. Callahan saw the new gold ring on her finger. His back came from the leather cushion as he reached across her.

"I'll tie the curtain back if you like."

"Thank you." He could just hear her over the chuckling of the sand-boxes and grinding tires.

He linked the ties. The sorghum odor of sage whipped at them. Broken foothills fenced the east, rising beyond a plain. They passed strings of freight wagons rumbling toward Reserve. On a far rise, Callahan glimpsed a raw cut where the railroad topped a mole-like ridge.

Her fingers meshed in her lap, Mrs. Winans suddenly said, "Mr. Callahan, I'd like to explain something. Mr. Hoagland is an old friend of my father's. I'm not interested in railroading, and I'm certainly not interested in—in Mr. Hoagland."

"You don't have to explain to me."

"You led me to think that I did."

"I'm sorry. I've had trouble with Hoagland. I was acting on the theory that any friend of his is an enemy of mine. Did Gentry tell you we have something in common?"

Her head turned. "Really?"

"We're both interested in buying into his line. And Mr. Hoagland won't care so much about that caper."

"You, too? Why?"

"I like horses."

"I see. My husband was in staging in California. He just died about two years ago."

"You married young," Callahan observed.

"I suppose."

"What did your husband die of?" Callahan's smile was a softness at the corners of his mouth.

His eyes watched her intently.

". . . They—they didn't—" She touched the bosom of her gown. "Pneumonia, they thought."

"A pity," Callahan sighed. "Hard to adjust, I know. Birthdays recall the departed . . . anniversaries. When was your anniversary, by the way?"

"The . . . the Fourth of July, I think," the girl said softly.

"Not sure?"

She pressed her lips together. "What are you trying to find out? What business is this of yours?"

"What you're trying to do. Wreck Gentry?"

Her eyes sparked. "I consider that a crude and—"

"I consider spying crude," Callahan said. "You're trying to get control of this stage-line. Then you'll sell the franchise to the railroad. Isn't that the whole deal in a nutshell?"

Her mouth was drab with fury or shock. Fire glinted in her eyes. "Except for disturbing the other passengers," she said, "I should slap you and ask that you be removed at the next station. We have nothing else to say to each other from now on."

"Except," Callahan sighed, "that it's too bad. There ought to be an ordinance against girls so pretty going into spying. Poor old Gentry. . . . He's being taken, hook, line and sinker."

2

THEY REACHED RIFLE HILL RELAY-STATION, WHERE A new team was latched into the traces. On they rolled, stopping for thirty minutes to lunch at Bridge Creek swing. The country was crumpling into higher hills gouged with canyons. Patches of timber birthmarked the tawny rimrock. Scented with the mountain incense of cedar and pine, the clear air was strapping.

Bill Fox, still chewing jerked venison, crawled to the box, and Gentry came around to the porch of the small station. "Ladies, will you take the inside seats?"

He escorted the three women to the coach. Then he spoke briefly to the men. "We pick up the military at Cross Hollows, eight mile from here. But this is all Injun country. I've seated the ladies away from the windows. None of you gents looks chicken-livered. Ain't, are you?"

He slapped on the back an assayer from Reserve, who

looked queasy, to Callahan, but tried to grin; chuckling, he went off to take his place atop the coach.

The coach slung along through dry washes and over hard-scrabble ridges. The going toughened. On the long grade descending into Cross Hollows Valley, they halted to rough-lock a rear wheel. Lurching on in a red fog of dust, they flattened into the shallow mountain valley. Near a black peninsula of timber running out into the basin, Callahan spotted the stage station. It was a brown box of log walls backed up by a couple of lean-to barns. A stack of wild hay was fenced off from deer and hungry stock. Two men were working with horses in a corral, and before the station were racked a dozen or more saddled horses. Fox's horn cried a bronze warning. The brakes squalled. Dust rolled by, cleared off, and Gentry was there to open the door.

"Twenty minutes," he said.

Callahan observed the men on the porch stare at the ladies as they entered the stage station. Sun and privation had been at them, scouring their bodies of fat, darkening their faces. They were a gaunt crew of volunteer Territorials, underpaid and underfed. Their shirts were a uniform pale-blue; hats, trousers and boots were catch-as-catch-can. A tall, sober man, slender and dark as a cheroot, came from the interior of the station. He wore a captain's bars on his shoulders.

"Your boys look gaunt," Gentry told him.

"We've been riding since dawn," the captain said.

Gentry introduced Callahan. "Captain Elmo Stanger," he said. They shook hands, Callahan noting the man's gray-black hair, a distinguishing note against his face, which was that of a man of thirty. Stanger was neat and precise and stern of eye and mouth. He held a fuming cigar and kept turning it in his fingers.

"What's up?" Gentry asked.

"Raid on the railroad camp yesterday afternoon. Three woodcutters were scalped. We've been on their tail all day. I make it twenty-thirty bucks."

"They come this way?"

"We're not here for the scenery."

Callahan noted a muscle tauten under the heavy flesh of Gentry's jaw. "I didn't expect you were," he said. "I expected you'd meet us here as I asked. But I'd like to know what to expect on the way in."

"Expect anything," Stanger said crisply. "You're on your own, by the way." He turned to the men. "Fall in!"

There was a too-quick scrambling. Callahan watched the cavalryman stride out to stand before the troopers. I'd hate to serve under you, he thought. I'd hate to soldier under any man who finds time to shave on patrol. Captain Stanger's jaws gleamed like cordovan.

Gentry knocked his pipe against his heel and walked out to take Stanger by the arm. "Say that once more."

A small fury pinched Stanger's face. "I can't give escort, that's what I mean! Pull off my men when we're about to close with the Utes? Lay over here, if you're afraid to proceed."

"Look good on my mail report, wouldn't it? 'Mail held up because of Injun scare.' "

"I don't care what it looks like. I'm serving the Territory, not the Colorado Express Company."

"Captain," Callahan said.

The troopers' faces turned his way. Stanger glanced about. "What is it?"

"We've got ladies aboard. It would hardly do to make them spend the night in Indian country, would it, when we can take them safely into town?"

"It's hard to say where the risk is greater," Stanger said. "But I can tell you I won't base my decision on what you or any other frightened stage passenger tells me."

He cracked an order at the cavalrymen. They broke for their horses. Callahan watched him, saying nothing. Gentry began to swear. "By God," he barked, "the governor will hear about this!"

Mounted, Stanger swung by them. "I hope he does, Gentry. Maybe we'd get decent subsidies for the railroad, then."

Fifteen minutes later the stagecoach ground back onto the country road, running smoothly with a fresh team across the valley. Reserve lay another thirty miles within the hills. The light was draining from the sky. In the dusty murk within the coach, Callahan took his Colt from the holster and laid it on his lap, under the skirt of his coat.

A finger touched his arm. Kathleen Winans was frowning at the half-obscured gun. "Do you have to do that?"

"I feel better doing it."

In a field of bright skunk-cabbage, they passed a freight outfit squared up for the night with the stock penned inside. Fires smoked and the wagon-master shook his head as they passed. A liver-spotted hound rushed the coach-team.

Fatigue invaded the coach. For nine hours the passengers had been pummeled and beaten by the brutalities of the road. Callahan's back was numb with rubbing against the horsehair cushions. His brain hummed. His head began to sag forward, and just as it seemed he was to get some rest, Roy Gentry's bass shout roused the whole coach.

"Keep 'er rolling!" Gentry yelled. "Gol-dang it, don't let her stop!" Thrusting his head out the window, Callahan saw a ruddiness on the flanks of the horses. Coming out of the turn, they swung left, out of his vision, and he had a clear view of the road. They were running into a bottleneck in a long valley, formed by a dike of sharply upstanding rocks. It was almost like a dam, rubbled at the base and sprinkled with aspen and small pine. The road burst through a gap in it, hardly twice the width of the coach itself. And the entire gap seemed to be afire.

The whole embrasure trembled with flame, yellow-

orange in the late sunset. It fell shatteringly on Callahan. Stupid with shock, he sat there with the long barrel
of his Colt resting on the ledge of the window.

Gentry's rifle rammed a black bolt of sound through
the air: It shattered into a scream against a rock. Fox's
soprano yelled:

"I can turn 'em, Roy!"

"Turn 'em, then, but don't slow!"

The coach left the graded roadbed and turned back.
It was in a rutted stand of spring grass, running bog-
gily, and the smoke of burning hay filled the coach. In
the florid light, Callahan saw the same face on all his
fellow-passengers: The dismal mask of fear.

Somewhere a gun cracked. He heard a ball strike the
leather belly of the coach, the deep luggage-boot behind him. Mrs. Winans fell across him as the coach
slewed over. She was sobbing.

Callahan locked his left arm about her. "Show those
Piutes something!" he said. He had no idea what. But
he made his arm steady and gripped the window with
the butt of his pistol.

All at once the air fluttered with arrows. They went
by like feathers. They thudded against the boot and a
horse screamed.

Gentry's rifle broke loose again. It was a heavy-
calibered Henry, a fifteen-shot wonder. Glancing out,
Callahan saw the Utes, jigging silhouettes against the
flames. Already the fire was lower, the hay burning
hotly. Callahan picked out a leader and tried to steady
the gun. It kicked at his wrist. The Indian kept coming.
He fired again, and as the smoke whipped away he saw
the riderless pony.

He lied in Mrs. Winans' ear: "Two of 'em, ma'am!"

The assayer was firing, now. Riding on the front seat,
he was able to fire into the Utes without twisting. The
coach filled with bitter fumes of powder. The Winans
girl pulled away, waxen.

"Can I do anything?"

"Shells in my pocket," Callahan said. "Extra guns under the seat."

He made the Colt slug thunderously across the meadow. Fanning out, the Indians showed their strength: There were at least two-dozen riders in fighting trim, shirtless, buffalo robes belted at the waist and flopping behind them. Feathered lances fluttered in the dark wind. In their shaggy, meagre ponies, Craig saw the only encouragement: A good stage team could outrun a poor saddle-horse in a fair race.

Gentry's carbine boomed steadily. The passengers made a crackling thunder with their side-arms. There was a pause while the stage-man reloaded. A moment later the coach swerved. It rocked through a sharp turn and struck back at the road. Kathleen Winans took Callahan's smoking Colt and gave him a fresh revolver. He studied the Indians milling on the road ahead of them, directly in the Concord's path. Gentry's gun opened again. It rolled and hammered as fast as one man could pull a lever and squeeze a trigger, and Callahan felt a glad lift: He saw several of the bunched warriors take the slugs, the whole group splitting, and when the Utes swerved away four horses ran without riders.

The hay had burned itself out: Callahan saw the fine silt of embers on the road. Smoke floated across the valley on the breeze. He felt the surge of the stage-ponies' gathered strength. The team was running wild.

Callahan pointed the barrel of the Colt at a group of riders to the right of the road. When they rushed, he was ready for them. They were like wild dogs snapping at the horses' legs. He fired until the gun clicked empty. He dropped it on the seat and Mrs. Winans was pressing another into his grip. The hard spine of the attack snapped. The Utes were in each other's way, trying to close and drive a lance into a pony or sink a feathered shaft. The passengers and the roaring madman atop the coach kept them off balance. Smoke whipped into the coach, the sweet smoke of burned hay.

Callahan fired until a slab of stone came between him and the Indians. The coach was through the gap. It was striking into a winding, easy grade up a hillside.

Watching the back road he suddenly knew the blood-feast was finished. The hangover had set in. Smoke and sunset curtained the gap in the broken stone wall. Presently Fox brought the horses into a trot.

An hour after sunset, her lamps gleaming, the stage-coach entered the canyon-town of Reserve. There was a sharpening quality in entering an almost-strange town at night, and Craig tilted his head to watch red-brick storefronts flash by, and the bright, steamy facades of saloons. The team minced into a narrow passage between two slot-like buildings and halted, blown, in a stage-yard. Hostlers took the nervous team and groped for harness snaps. A limping baggage man unbuckled the flap of the rear boot.

Finally Gentry was alone with the Winans girl and Callahan. He smiled ruefully. "Investor line forms at the right," he said.

"I'd like to be first in that line," the girl said.

"You'll have to stand on my shoulders to get there," Callahan said. "That was only the acid test, Gentry: You've got a real stage line."

Gentry wagged his head. "Then I reckon you're both crazy. Well, it's late. Callahan, I've got a spare room you can share with the rats. Mrs. Winans, I'll find you a room. The Mountain House is good."

"I'd like a suite, if there is such a thing," Mrs. Winans said. "You know, a little sitting room I can use for an office."

Callahan was weary. He picked up his trunk, balanced it on his shoulder and said, "You load a Colt with the best, ma'am. We'll take on the Sioux Nation some time."

"Not if I can help it. Good-night, Mr. Callahan." She turned her back to him.

In the room, Callahan lay on the cot with his long

legs falling over the side. The red brick walls absorbed
the weak candle light. The lurch and sag of the stagecoach were still in him. He slept. When he awoke, the
candle was a curl of black twine in a puddle of grease.
He lay thinking that he was lucky to be here at all; the
thought led into bitter recollection of Captain Elmo
Stanger. He recalled the faces of his men—like a pack
of hungry hounds. It would be pleasant to have the upper hand with him, just once.

Mrs. Winans had taken it well. Scared, but hanging
on. In the cold dusk of the room he projected her im-
age: How she had looked coming out of Hoagland's
room . . . how she had said, "Mr. Hoagland is an old
friend of my father's. . . ."

And of yours, Miss Kitty, thought Callahan.

It was the core of a hard problem. Gentry should
know she was on the railroad's payroll, that she was
Hoagland's woman and trying to trap him. It was only
fair to him as well as to Gentry. But he could not go to
Gentry with what he knew. He could not do it. Admit-
ting that, he uncovered the edge of a hurt in himself.
An impersonal hurt, perhaps—that any girl so attractive
could have such morals. It made a man want to regard
all women in the same light. If you could not believe
in one like her, what kind could you believe in?

With a grunt, he came off the cot and poured water
in a graniteware bowl from a wooden bucket. Refreshed
and brushed, he consulted his watch. Nine-thirty. He
ran a cleaning rag down the barrel of his Colt, reloaded
with care and left the room.

In the baggage room, behind the ticket office, he encountered a dozen stage men listening to Bill Fox
drunkenly reciting an Indian story. Callahan perceived
something: Gentry was living in the past, in the golden
era of staging. He had surrounded himself with old men
from the Oxbow Route, the Birch lines, the Central
Overland. Laid end to end, the years of these twelve
men would reach back halfway to Nero.

". . . damned if a mule wasn't down in the traces," Fox was chattering. He snatched the knife from his boot. "I told my guard, 'Hold 'em!' and I clumb down. Arrows thicker'n fleas on a dog's back!"

Passing Gentry, Callahan murmured, "Like a drink?"

Gentry took his hat and they went outside. A fine mountain mist had descended suddenly from the crags. The brick fronts of the buildings shone wetly. A slate church steeple prodded the mist. "National Saloon serves the freshest hard-boil' eggs," said the stage man. "Whiskey's about the same everywhere."

They walked upstreet a block. Wagons and rigs jogged past. Most of the business houses seemed to be assayers' laboratories, trading on the avalanche of ore samples from the mines. Of brick and volcano tuffa, the town looked rich and permanent.

Callahan was suddenly aware of a phenomenon at the hitch rack of the National Saloon. Gentry, too, must have seen it, for he hesitated. In the golden haze drifting before the saloon's big window stood a line of horses, dull with road dirt, each bearing a blanket roll behind the cantle.

"I don't know," Gentry growled. "Lot of railroad bums be drinking there, this being Saturday night. Let's try the Palace."

It was difficult to think of the stage man in the same instant with lack of courage. But Callahan knew the horses were those of Captain Stanger's squadron. ". . . You've got me honing for those hard-boiled eggs," he said.

The oval glass doors of the National swung in. In a smoky distance, a mirrored wheel spun and a girl cried the bets. A mechanical piano and drum roared through, *When Johnny Comes Marching Home*, and girls and red-shirted miners shuffled behind a rope enclosure. The heavy walnut bar was backed with a glittering display of crystal. An impartial rail supported the boots of miners, freighters and business men, and Callahan saw a row of cavalry-spurred boots and followed them up to the exhausted, unshaven faces of the troopers. They had been here only a short while; dark yokes of moisture lay across their shoulders. At a table near the slowly-clicking wheel, he located Captain Stanger. The officer sat with a blond, thick-set man and a full-bosomed girl in a flounced dress.

"Let's pay our respects to the captain," Callahan told Gentry.

Gentry shook his head. "We'd be mobbed to hell and back if we tackled him and Braga."

Callahan had not recognized the old T. & A. work boss, Tom Braga. Now he saw the thick, creased neck rising into the tough blond hair, the flat ears and massive shoulders of the man. He watched the pair talk, Stanger gravely amused at something Braga was telling him. Wandering, the captain's eyes came to a sudden collision with Callahan's. Callahan absently removed his hat, ran his hand over his hair, and replaced it, not moving his eyes from the officer's face.

He said, "You know what to do about railroad towns, don't you? Lick a couple of good railroad men and then take it over . . ."

He went down the line of cocked hips at the bar, turning out through the tables to lay a hand on Braga's shoulder. Braga twisted to look up at him.

"Tom, how's the junk business?" Callahan asked.

Stanger's dark, sober face watched him, and the girl laughed softly.

Braga grinned. "Sit down, Craig. Got your message. Junk business is booming. . . . How're the horse manure kings of Colorado?"

"Well, we don't try to fool anybody about what we're selling."

Callahan took a chair but Gentry said, "Craig, I've got to see to the stock. Side door'll be open."

Callahan looked at him. Gentry looked troubled, but

kept his anger toward Stanger and Braga turned inward . . . as, Craig supposed, he had done with Hoagland from the start; and that was how they had managed to back him into this corner. "All right," he said.

"I heard you ran into some trouble today," Braga remarked. His eyes absently touched a scar above Callahan's right eyebrow, where the railroad man's own fist had broken the skin once. But Craig could not find a mark on Braga. The construction boss had a tough, masculine good looks, a man's-man handsomeness—heavy in the jaw, his eyes blue and seasoned with lines, a humorous mouth that never lost its good nature, even when a gauger had to be whipped for improperly spotting a half-mile of rails. Braga held a shot glass in his right hand; his sleeves were rolled, and the hairs on his forearms gleamed golden.

"Trouble? A little," Callahan said. "The worst was having women with us."

Stanger said, "Don't say you weren't warned."

"We were given a choice of evils. That was what the military did for us."

As she raised her drink, the girl smiled at Callahan. "If we'd been properly introduced, I'd ask you to bring me a scalp next time."

She was with the captain, Callahan saw, not with Braga. He had not intended to introduce her, but now he said, "Callahan, is it? Shawn Miller, Callahan."

Callahan gallantly rose and bent over the hand she extended. She was a bold and attractive auburn-haired girl, probably not twenty. She had a pouting lower lip and wore dangling gold crosses as earrings; and Callahan hoped she took them off when she worked.

"It may not be too late yet to get you a scalp," he said. "Any preference as to color?"

Her dark, humorous eyes went to his own black hair. "Black is nice," she said. " 'Black is the color of my true love's hair' . . ."

"Shawn," Stanger snapped, "we've got business to talk." He put his hand on the back of her chair.

"How many Indians did you kill, Mr. Callahan?" Shawn asked.

"Three."

"Your first?"

"Yes. We usually have a military escort in dangerous country. I think our escort was off on railroad business somewhere."

"Why, Elmo!" Shawn exclaimed. "Weren't you to bring the stage in today?"

Stanger's face darkened. He leaned forward, his glass held between his fingertips. "Will you keep your civilian nose out of military matters?" he asked Callahan.

"Why didn't you tell me he was touchy?" Callahan asked Shawn.

"Sometimes he's terrible," she said. "But then, sometimes he's sweet." She put her hand over Stanger's, who drew it away.

Braga leaned back. "You mean we'd bribe a military man to neglect his duty?"

"That's how it used to be worked. Troops to guard the woodcutters, while freighters were murdered ten miles away."

The headlong music of the piano had resumed. Rising, Callahan looked at Stanger but extended a hand to Shawn. "I expect Miss Miller is off-limits to civilian personnel too, eh, Captain?"

As the girl rose, Stanger said, "Shawn—sit down."

But she was coming into Callahan's arms, her face tilted to smile at him. They moved away to the roped dancing enclosure. Callahan saw Stanger sitting at the table, staring at his drink, and Braga's mouth said something bitter to the officer; something biting.

"Don't you care whether you live to be an old man or not?" Shawn asked him. They elbowed into the pack of flounced dancing girls and intent miners.

"Not if I can spend my youth like this," Callahan grinned.

Shawn laughed softly. "You don't like my friend."

"No," agreed Craig.

"So," she pouted, "you dance with me to make him mad."

"Let's put it this way: If there were ten pretty girls in the room, and Stanger was with one of them, I'd dance with that one. But I didn't expect to draw the prettiest."

"You know," Shawn sighed, "I'd rather be lied to by a man like you than have a man like—well, any other man, tell me the truth."

"That makes two good liars in this couple, doesn't it?"

The professor wove a last tinkling run and reached for his beer. Leaving the floor, Shawn asked, "Married, Craig?"

"Not even a steady."

"Need a steady?"

"Only for tonight."

"That's too bad. I could have any miner in town, and I don't mean suckers. I could even have a cavalry captain. Or your friend, Braga, if I wanted him."

"Then what do you like about me?"

"Maybe I like the fact that they're both afraid of you," she told him.

At the table, she folded her hands, smiled brightly at Braga, then at the captain, and said, "Somebody took my drink."

"More on the way," Braga said. He squinted at Callahan. "So you came out to lick us. All by yourself?"

"No. I've got helpers. Several thousand of them."

Braga looked puzzled. Leaning back, Callahan looked for the waiter. The man was coming through the crowd. At this moment, Stanger arose. "Shawn, come along." Emotion darkened his lean face.

"I haven't had my drink."

"I'll buy you one at the bar, damn it!" Stanger said.

The barman was there, then, setting down glasses, and Callahan was taking something from his hip pocket, a folded packet of engraved pages.

Braga's face was rough with headlong fury. "Put those away!" he snapped.

Callahan took one of the papers from the packet and handed the rest to the waiter. "Ten dollars if you'll pin those up behind the bar," he said. "And put a notice under them: 'For Sale—Bonds in Texas and Arkansas Railroad. Sold at $50. Special this week, 50¢.' That's about the going rate," he explained.

Braga put one hand on the table and one on the arm of his chair. "Give them here, mister," he said quietly.

Shawn took the bond certificate from Craig's hand. "Pretty," she said. "What are they?"

"Bonds," he said. "Bonds that went to build Marsh Hoagland's last road, the T. & A. I helped build it, God help me, and so did Tom Braga. And now neither of us can enter the state of Texas again without being locked up. And tomorrow I'll tell Reserve about it."

Braga stood over him, a muscular, hard-eyed man with his fists balled. "You'll tell them it's a lie," he said. "A damned, jealous lie, because you weren't cut in on this job. I could have tromped you that night, Callahan. Once or twice I've been sorry I didn't."

"You aren't going to tromp me, though, Tom," Callahan said, "and you don't build another scrap-iron railroad."

It was not apparent that he had moved. But Braga swore and doubled at the belt. Craig had smashed his heel down on the construction man's instep. He came up, then, while Braga was recovering, his fist rising under the man's face and smashing into his mouth. Braga stumbled back, caught himself on a chair, and hesitated just long enough to wipe his bleeding mouth. Then his hand snapped down and he slammed the chair aside and lunged back.

3

CALLAHAN WAITED, DARK-SKINNED, A SLIVER OF
smile showing between his lips. The saloonkeeper was
coming from somewhere. "Now, boys!" he shouted.
Braga was in with a smashing swing at Craig's jaw, the
breath whistling through his teeth. Swerving away, Callahan felt the edge of the blow against his ear. Braga
went by and Callahan pivoted to catch him. He missed
with an overhand right and stepped into the man with
a left. The blow thumped against Braga's chest.

Braga coughed and spat blood in Craig's face. Suddenly his knee rose toward Craig's crotch. As Craig
ducked, he clamped a hammer-lock about the taller
man's neck and brought his head down. Locking it
against his ribs, he commenced smashing his left fist
against the back of Callahan's neck. Hurt, Craig fought
in blind shock. He was hammering at the railroad man's
kidneys; he could feel the tough back-muscles under his
fist. Braga was a chunk of gristle, as hard to grapple as

a stump. The man was a competitor, a fighter all the way through.

Callahan suddenly plowed forward and they came up against the piano. Sawdust slid beneath their bootsoles. They were going down. Something cold drenched his face. He felt the cold skin of a schooner against his neck. As Braga's grip loosened, he yanked away. Braga was on his back with his head on the pedals, swearing, and Callahan came to his knees and struck at the bloody, furious face. He saw a cut open in a crisp blond eyebrow. Braga tried to roll. Callahan sat on his legs and slashed again at the cut. It gaped, and blood puddled about Braga's eye. Braga had the beer-schooner, suddenly. Craig seized his wrist to keep him from cocking for a blow.

They rolled away from each other as the schooner fell. Crouching, then, Callahan watched the man lurch up. He rose almost from Braga's feet, slashing at his eye again. Braga's head rolled. He pulled a chair to him; abruptly it went up over his head, his short arms bent. Callahan backed away. He heard the crowd bawling at them. He heard a girl laughing hysterically and wondered whether it was Shawn. Then he felt the bar at his back. Braga was still coming on. Callahan's right hand went out along the bar, hunting something to throw; he dared not take his eyes off the railroad man. His fingers encountered the icy side of a cut-glass bowl. They fumbled up the side and closed on the edge. Something smooth, round and cold brushed his fingers; suddenly he had a desire to laugh. He pulled the bowl to him as Braga moved in and seized a handful of hard-boiled eggs, the best hard-boiled eggs in town, Roy Gentry had said.

Braga ducked as the first eggs flew. They struck the mirrored wheel with small crunching sounds. The second salvo missed him and hit the piano. A man began to roar with laughter. The third hit Tom Braga in the face. He was half-blind with particles of smashed yolk.

He suddenly drove forward, and Callahan threw the bowl. It hit Braga's head just as he swung the chair. Callahan slid from under it and came at the railroad man from the side as the chair crashed against the mahogany.

Braga wheeled, his eyes slow and puzzled. At his hair-line there was a deep and ghastly cut the width of a man's hand, just commencing to bleed. Abruptly his knees loosened, but he recovered with two staggering steps and veered into Craig with a violent side-arm swing. Callahan drew his right arm and the massed power of his back and shoulder drove his fist levelly into Braga's jaw. Braga's eyes closed. His head was turned by the thrust of Callahan's fist. He stumbled sidewards. As he toppled, a man tried to support him, but he fell heavily in the sawdust.

After a moment Callahan's shoulders sagged. He shook his head and turned to the bar. The saloonkeeper stood there, impotently gripping a side-hammer shotgun. "Somebody's going to pay for this, or live on jail grub for a month."

"I call on Shawn to witness that he swung first," said Craig. "Charge it to the railroad crowd. But don't let them pay off in bonds."

He started down the bar, vaguely aware of the men silently watching him. He let his hand touch the back of each chair he passed, steadyingly. Someone was beside him.

"You can't go anywhere like that, Craig," Shawn Miller said. "You come with me. My room is upstairs." Slipping her arm through his, she piloted him to the front. On the street, the mist was colder, lowering and wet over the heavy street traffic. They started around the building to the sheet-metal outside stairway. A man and woman came out of the musty fog. It was a moment before Callahan realized it was Kathleen Winans and Roy Gentry. Gentry was carrying the girl's bags and saying,

"Got a promise on this suite as soon as somebody checked out tonight. You might have to wait a few minutes . . ."

They saw Callahan, then. He was bloody. He could feel the slow worming of a stream of blood from his nose. He weaved a little. Impatiently, Shawn gave his arm a shake.

"What's wrong, Craig? Can't you make it?"

Mrs. Winans' eyes opened widely. She winced at the blood on him. She stared at the saloon girl, in her short, flounced green dress. Then her glance dropped and she took Gentry's arm hastily. "I think we should hurry."

"Oh, they wouldn't dast—" At this point Gentry saw Callahan. "Craig, what the jasus—!"

"You were right," said Callahan. "This was a railroad town. But we've started making it over."

Shawn's room was a cell-like chamber at the end of a dim hall. She made him sit on a chair while she cleaned his cuts and tore up strips of cloth. The walls were covered with a dismal brown paper. Overhead, a carbide light fizzed. There was a display of rigid ambrotypes on a dresser. Callahan saw a gray military hat, the brim up on one side, hanging from a poster of the brass bedstead.

She saw him regarding it. Petulantly, she snatched it from the bed and threw it in the hall. "A man who would take that!"

She gave him a drink. Afterward, he got up. His head was musty with unassorted thoughts. How Kitty had looked . . . the feel of his fist on Braga's jaw—"Thanks, Shawn," he said. "I'll buy you a drink sometime."

"You'll buy me a lot of drinks," she told him, smiling.

Callahan shook his head. "I said I only needed a steady for tonight. If I needed one, though, I'd know where to find her."

Later, then, lying in his own room, he thought: This

could get complicated, mister. Let's watch the angles from here on.

Sometime during the evening, a letter had been dropped in the slot of the stage company door. In the morning, it was lying there in a box with a few other pieces of mail.

"Mr. Hollis Lamerick would appreciate a conference with Mr. Craig Callahan at eleven o'clock at the San Juan County Bank."

He had expected something like this, and at eleven o'clock, shaven, his face cuts adjusted by a barber, he entered the bank. Next door, he saw the main office of the Far-Western Railroad Company. Unaware that space was all they had plenty of, Colorado people, he had noticed, had a tendency to build their structures high and narrow. This one was like a high-ceilinged hall. It was covered with pseudo-mahogany paper and carpeted with linoleum, pitted by the hobnails of miners and freighters. There were dust scales back of a spindly railing. A vault yawned, and before it was a desk inhabited by a stout man in a brown suit. A thin, ascetic-looking man sat with him. Both were smoking cigars, and appeared gloomy. A clerk took Callahan inside the railing.

"Mr. Sizemore, our manager," he introduced the stout man. "And Mr. Lamerick."

Callahan accepted a cigar. "Excuse the scars, gentlemen. I was brawling last night."

Lamerick cleared his throat with a bleating sound. He looked to Callahan like a pale and elderly Indian. His nose was lean and his eyes were cavernous and piercing. There was not a hint of humor in him.

"Is that the only way you know to adjust a difference, Callahan?" he asked.

"No. They use a gun, in Texas."

"They use a gun in Colorado, too, when it comes to it." Sizemore, the banker, said. "When the people of

Reserve know what you're trying to do, it may come to it very quickly.''

"What *am* I trying to do?" Callahan asked.

"Break the town, along with Far-Western Railroad Company. Reserve is saturated with railroad bonds. The bank alone holds a hundred and fifty thousand dollars worth. Every waitress and stablehand has bought.''

"Is that my worry?''

Sizemore's eyes were a muddy-brown. He turned the fuming cigar in his fingers. "Only if you try to halt construction. I suppose Gentry told you I hold an overdue note of his?''

Callahan grunted. "Threats. I thought you had an offer to make me.''

Lamerick said bitterly, "I thought you might be a bonafide staging man. Go ahead with your plan to buy in with Gentry, if an offer is what you want. We'll take the stock off your hands later.''

"If I get the stock, there won't be enough money in Reserve to buy it away from me. How did he sucker you men into this? You've tied up with a man who's been blackballed from the railroad trade. He can't go back to Texas, where he built a road two years ago. Neither can I, because I was his assistant engineer. The road fell apart. And so will this one.''

Lamerick smiled. "In mining towns," he said, "you hear a lot of wild stories. This is one of the best I've heard.''

Callahan pulled a T. & A. bond certificate from his pocket and laid it on the desk. "Wire the capitol about this. There's Hoagland's picture in the corner. I didn't quite make the grade, myself. Thank God for that!''

The men looked at it. The edge of a doubt showed for an instant in Lamerick's puckered blue eyes. Then he snorted. "I didn't quit banking to be badgered into bankruptcy by a medicine-show financier. I think that's all we have to say to each other.''

The phrase had a familiar ring; it was like a known

voice distantly heard. And then through all the stiffness of bearing, Callahan saw something in Hollis Lamerick, and he chuckled.

"All right, Lamerick. But let's not talk about medicine show tactics. One that I've been watching is about to break, too. I think we'll have something to say to each other, after that."

There was a small office behind the waiting room of the stage station. At a pyre of coals on a tiny hearth, Kathleen Winans knelt to warm her fingers. Callahan sat in a chair propped against the wall.

Gentry had sent for Mrs. Winans, at the hotel, and caught Craig after lunch. "No use fussin' around. You've seen the road and equipment. The books are here. I operate four coaches, figger fifteen hundred apiece. Figger hosses at a hundred each; that's seventy-six hundred. Figger miscellaneous equipment at another two thousand. Come to around thirteen thousand, not includin' good will. Knock it down to ten for depreciation."

"Clear?" asked Callahan.

"You didn't think I'd sell stock if it was, did you? I've lost money on the mail contract the last three years."

Kitty kept her face turned to the fire. "How much for fifty-one percent?"

"A million dollars. For forty-nine percent, three thousand. That would clear me."

"I'll give you thirty-two," said Callahan.

"Thirty-five!" Kathleen said sharply. She stood, her hands clenched.

"Thirty-six."

Gentry scratched his neck. "Let's have one thing clear: Stock will be non-transferable. I'll have no railroad scum for a pardner."

Callahan's ears warmed; but Gentry was regarding Kitty Winans. "I've heard that Callahan—begging his pardon—used to work for Tom Braga and Marsh Hoagland. I heard that he knocked the tar out of Braga last night. Does that mean," he asked, "that you're shut of railroading?"

"A straight answer for a straight question: No. But it means I'll make you a rich man when I ram this stageline down their throats."

Gentry's mouth hardened. "I wouldn't have the Union Pacific railroad itself as a present."

Craig locked his hands behind his back. "I'll gamble I can talk you into selling to them, when the time comes. If I can't, it's my loss, not yours. On the other hand, you'd have trouble getting that money anywhere else. I heard a note of yours was about to be called by Sizemore."

"Of course, there's still Mrs. Winans," Gentry observed. "You ain't saying much, Kitty. I've kind of been thinking of you as my pardner."

Callahan saw how pale she had gone. Her face was set. "I—I hoped it could be that way."

"Because I know I can count on you," Gentry said. "I know your background, and I figure staging is a better place to be from than railroading."

Kitty Winans' eyes suddenly filled. "Stop it!" she said. She took a step toward him, and then snatched her cape from a wall-hook. "I've just remembered something. I—I can't do it."

Callahan moved to lean back against the door, smiling as he blocked her escape. "You just remembered your name was Lamerick, didn't you?"

The cape fell from Kitty's fingers. Her eyes were wide. Callahan stopped to retrieve the cape. When he straightened, she had walked to Gentry.

"You knew, too, didn't you?"

Gentry smiled. "I'd hate to say that you looked like an old goat like Hollis Lamerick, but there *is* something."

She turned back. At the door, she faced them. "But this much is the truth: I made them promise you'd make money out of it. They said you'd be paid well, in money and stock. And of course the stage line *can't* last long, Mr. Gentry.''

''That's where we disagree,'' Gentry said quietly.

She opened the door. ''I'm sorry. For everything. And I'd like to say something to you, too, Mr. Callahan—something you said to me. I don't think your friends are the best in the world, either.''

Callahan said gravely, ''I'd pick better, Kitty, if I had any encouragement.''

She turned and walked briskly from the room.

''Nice young woman,'' Gentry sighed. ''But I knew from the first she was no stagin' woman. Why, hell, she called the tugs 'thorough-braces' once! Well,'' he said, ''if you want to throw money around thataway, let's walk up to the bank.''

4

AFTERWARD, THEY SIGNED PAPERS AT A LAWYER'S OF-
fice, and shook hands on the boardwalk. The chill of
early evening stung the thronged street. A jackass train
jingled past and a couple of gopher-hole miners rode
by on mules.

Gentry looked at his watch. "By damn! That stage
is due."

"Go on down," Callahan said. "I'm going to drop
in on Judge Lightfoot. I sounded him on your chances
to make that franchise stick when I was up here before.
He promised me a cease and desist when I ask for it.
I'm asking for it now."

Gentry hesitated. "Good luck. Understand one thing,
Craig. Anytime you want to see fireworks, you furnish
your own matches. I figure I can lick them without making
a fuss. If you want to stand up and beller—go ahead."

After a moment Craig said, "Suppose there's trouble. Whose side will you be on?"

Gentry's eyes hardened. "I'm on the side of the Colorado Stage Company. Let them touch one of my stagecoaches, or one of my drivers, and they've got a scrap on. Being that you ain't a coach or a driver, Callahan, you're on your own."

He turned and strode down the walk toward the depot. Callahan watched his suspendered back disappear into the crowd. Then he ascended the steep, curving street to the county courthouse.

In his shadowy chambers behind the courtroom, Judge Cady Lightfoot seated Callahan and swung an extension-lamp over his desk. A bearded man of fifty, he was stout as a bull and roared everything he said. "Hearing things about you, Callahan!" he declared. "Whipped Tom Braga, did you?"

"I always said I could," said Callahan.

Lightfoot grabbed in a desk drawer. "From what I gather, you won't have to do it again. They took him out to the railroad camp in a wagon. Here we are. Reckoned you'd be back, so I drawed it up."

He adjusted pince-nez spectacles, turned up the lamp-flame, and read the instrument aloud. He affixed his name, vised his official seal onto the document and handed it to Callahan.

"And that," he said, "was the start of the damndest fight you ever saw! It'll take more than paper and ink to block Far-Western."

"You don't think I can scare them, eh?"

"I don't think anybody can scare Marsh Hoagland. He was in here once threatening to have me impeached if I ever signed such a document as that-there. I said I'd have him arrested for attempted intimidation. He laughed in my face."

Callahan went to the door but Lightfoot spoke again. "Got it in for railroads, have you?"

"Just this one."

"That's too bad," sighed the judge. "I happen to hold ten thousand dollars worth of their bonds. It was my duty to sign that paper, but it's my own business if I hope they knock the tar out of you. Good-night.''

The mountain darkness had fallen like a blanket. Callahan lingered to light a cigar before starting down the street. He was abreast of the alley between the courthouse and a carriage factory when a man spoke beside him.

"Why don't you just serve it here?"

Callahan halted. He did not turn immediately; it might be the man held a gun, and it was possible he was nervous. Then he recorded the voice. "I could do that, Marsh," he said.

Hoagland stood there with another man, who was lean and dark and wore a cavalryman's hat. It was Captain Elmo Stanger. Hoagland wore a heavy corduroy coat and flat Stetson. His face was blocked out in shadow. A gun glinted darkly in his hand.

"Walk down the alley," Hoagland said. "Ahead of us."

"Maybe I should scream," Callahan suggested.

"Maybe you should try."

Reaching the far end, they were on a quiet back street behind the business section. A man on each side of him, they started down the hill. "When do I get to serve the paper?" Callahan asked. His eyes flicked ahead of them.

"This is it," Stanger said. The cavalryman opened a rear door. Preceding them, Stanger lighted a lamp. Shades were drawn in the front office. It was a large, bare room with maps on the wall, mapcases forming a partition between front and rear portions, and several desks on an oiled wood floor. This was the office of the railroad company. Hoagland now took Callahan's .45 and patted his clothing for the belly-gun he had used before.

Craig stared at the cavalryman. "Where do you come into this, General?"

"I come into this in keeping the peace. You've set out to disrupt everything in sight. It goes beyond town jurisdiction. It becomes mine, when you tamper in territorial matters."

"Or romantic?"

Hoagland pulled a chair and sat near Callahan, drawing a billfold from his coat. "That was a hell of a licking you gave Tom Braga," he remarked. "You always said you could."

"If you're superstitious, you should be sweating. I said I could lick you, too."

"I'm not," said Hoagland. "Tom wanted to come back and kill you. I told him not to be a damned fool. You'd had your fun, and you'd be ready to clear out, now, and it would look like you were afraid of him coming back at you. So he could still strut."

"I haven't had all my fun, though."

"You've had the part that's going to be fun." Hoagland handed him the same bond certificate he had given Hollis Lamerick that morning. "My partner handed me this when I came in tonight. Got any more of them?"

"A trunkful."

"That's what I figured. How much do you want for them?"

"A job. In charge of construction for Far-Western."

Hoagland's face acquired a look of dry anger, a crowding impatience. "You'll sit there with a gun on you and talk like the same damned fool you always were! The Robin Hood of railroading. Get it into your head that I'm building this road! That you've had your party and now you're going to clean up the mess."

He threw the certificate at a wastebasket. From the billfold, he tugged a draft. He snapped it taut with his fingers. "Five thousand dollars," he said. "That gives you a profit. I got it that you paid thirty-six hundred. That'll buy your way out."

"What good would forty-nine percent do you?"

"A lot. Even a forty-nine percent partner can do a lot of ordering of things the company don't need. He can drag his feet till the whole outfit comes to a stop. Don't think a franchise is concrete, either, mister. It can be broken. But understand this: You've shot off your mouth around here for the last time. You got Lamerick riled up. He was preaching to me like a Sunday school superintendent. What had I done, and what was all this about being banned in Texas? I'll take no more of it, from you or from any-body. I warned you to keep out of it.''

He wadded the check and threw it to Callahan, who caught it. Hoagland said, ''Stanger will take you to the county line.''

Callahan looked over the whiplike cavalryman, noting the bottled anger in his face. ''Does he guarantee safe-conduct?''

''That's between you and him,'' said Hoagland.

''You don't go about things like a man who cared what happened to him, anyway,'' Stanger said. ''I might have killed you the other night.''

''Why didn't you?''

''How would it look—an officer squabbling in a saloon?''

''It would look better than crawfishing.''

Callahan put the balled check on the lamp chimney, where it browned and caught fire, sending a tall column of flame upward. ''You didn't try,'' he said, ''because you're yellow. And Hoagland comes around after dark because he's yellow. And I'll be damned if I can't lick both of you!''

They were moving in, Stanger's gun still watching him, but Craig's palm smashed the cut-glass reservoir of the lamp and it arched toward the cavalryman. He ducked and slashed at the lamp, holding his fire. Landing, it crashed into blackness.

Hoagland was lunging at him through the darkness. Callahan ducked out of the chair. He struck a mapcase with his shoulder and it began to topple. Something mashed his ear painfully. He heard the case strike the floor. He was down and rolling over and coming up, and a dark shape was over him and slashing at his head. He sank down, pressing his palms against the sides of his head.

Even then, instinct drove him away again. Captain

Stanger was feinting in; in the darkness, diluted by a
street light, he groped after Callahan with one hand,
his other raised. Craig fired a blow at his groin. He
heard him cry out. He charged after him with both
hands, crawling over broken glass as he went. Stanger
fell under him.

A clap of sound shook the room. For an instant they were
all included in a bloody sphere of light. Hoagland was
groping about, bent at the waist, a revolver palmed in his
right hand, as a club. Stanger's face was waxy—his lips
were pulled back from his teeth, his eyes stared crazily as
Callahan's fingers hunted the Colt he had fired.

The instant died. Hoagland was rushing in. As Callahan began to twist at the gun, the railroad boss
smashed at his head. It was a staggering thing which
lasted only a moment. It was pain drenching him darkly,
and flowing away, and then a vast ocean of ease.

You could die like this, he thought, and nobody would
know or give a damn. You could regain your senses
with blood glueing your head to the floor, with your
skull expanding and contracting like a concertina—you
could crawl to the door and lie there making sounds
when someone walked past, but you might as well be
on the prairie. You were alone.

But he was alive. That was surprising. It was only
that no one liked to do murder; murder was the most
inefficient system of disposal in the world. You could
whip a man out of town and no one would care. But if
you killed him, someone, sometime, would want to
know about it.

Heels tapped past the door again and he rolled onto
his side and tried to reach the door to strike at it. His
knuckles missed by inches. But the footfalls turned in.
A key rasped in a padlock and the door swung in and
bumped his shoulder. He moaned.

Kitty Winans uttered a short and startled scream. She
retreated. He could see her bell-like silhouette against the
light of the street. A turn-out ground past, but did not stop.

Callahan mumbled: "Kitty . . ."

"Craig," Kitty said; her voice was low, accusing, and tragic.

In the lamplight she helped him sit up. She bustled, with constant exclamations. "I never, never, *never* saw a man who— No! Sit there."

Suddenly it dawned on her. She stood, her mouth open, staring at him as he tried to keep his chin from touching his chest. "You were robbing the office? Someone must have—"

He waved a hand. "Get me a drink."

She found something. He let the brandy feather the edge from his nerves and moved to a chair.

"The more I see of your friends," he said, "the less I think of them. When I get Stanger alone—"

"Stanger? He's your friend, not mine. Or his girl is, from what I was able to gather last night."

"She was just taking me to her room to fix me up."

"And tonight I'm the lucky girl."

"Kitty," he said, "do you want to know what happened?"

"Do you want to tell me?"

"Hoagland and Stanger licked me. The two of them."

Her features firmed. "Mr. Hoagland isn't that kind."

"When the time comes," Craig said, "he'll have someone hold your father's arms behind him, and he'll beat him until he agrees to whatever Hoagland wants. That's what they did to me in Texas."

Kitty turned away and stood at the door, staring out. "I don't believe it, Craig. I don't think my father is so poor a judge of men as that."

"I didn't think I was, either."

He drank more of the brandy. He could feel drying blood crack on his neck when he tilted his head. "Do me a favor. Go get Gentry. He'll get me home."

"All right. Craig," she said, turning to him, "was

that bond certificate legitimate? Is that really Mr. Hoag-land's picture on it?''

"If I told you he licked me because I wouldn't turn the rest of them over to him, you wouldn't believe me. So let's say it was George Washington.''

"You've upset Father," she confessed. "He wired Texas. But we know what the answer will be. You're bluffing.''

"I'm a poor bluffer. Only women bluff well.''

She stood close to him, shaking her head. "As long as you live you'll think of me as a liar and a cheat.''

Callahan shook his head. "As long as I live, Kitty, I'll wonder why we had to meet this way. On opposite sides of the fence.''

Callahan slept, aided by liquor. He awoke to a warm morning. He could see horses tugging at heaps of hay in the corral. A workman was filing a horse's hoof, its foreleg gripped between his knees. But the usual morning sight of Gentry washing down a stagecoach was absent. Callahan had an outsize headache. He attempted to get out of bed, but had to give up.

He slept again, and afterward Gentry came with a steaming cup of coffee. He sat making sounds with his plates while Callahan told him about his session with Hoagland and Captain Stanger.

"Stanger took off this morning for end-o'-track with fifteen troopers," Gentry growled. "That's practically his whole command. Ain't seen Hoagland. I tried to get Stanger to check on that coach. Last night's mail didn't come in. I could be sore at you, Callahan," he said. "Things were going all right. At least they left me alone.''

"They wouldn't raid a mail-coach!" Callahan exclaimed. "Hell, that's Federal property.''

"Maybe Piutes raided it. Maybe Hoagland bought them the whiskey and pointed out where to knock it over. I'll give it till tonight," he said. "Then I'm going out. No freight's come in, either. I don't savvy it.''

Callahan lay staring at the ceiling. "That's only eighteen hours. Might be a washout.''

"Been no storm," said Gentry. "I'll leave you in charge of the office if I go. Can you handle it without getting in a gunfight?"

Through that day Callahan rested. He heard men in front demanding mail. Once a man said:

"Wait'll that train's a-runnin', you old mossback! We'll have daily service, and on time, by God!"

There was a side door to his room, which opened onto the yard. Near sundown the porcelain knob turned, and Callahan saw the door slowly slant in. He was lying on his side at the time, a cigar in his mouth. In an instant he had his Colt in his hand. He watched stiffly while the door swung into the room.

A girl's face showed in the dusk. Suddenly she saw the gun. "Craig!"

It was Shawn Miller. Callahan shoved the gun back under his pillow.

She sat on the edge of the bed, wincing as she looked at him. "I didn't think he was man enough to do it. He told me this morning he'd whipped you. I thought he was lying. But I had to see."

"Stanger? He's *mucho hombre*," said Craig. "With somebody holding my arms."

Her eyes held a dark shine. "Was it that way?"

"That's the way I remember it."

"If I were a man," she breathed, "and anyone did that to me—!"

"Do you want me to give it back to him?" He watcher her, amused.

"He's a coward," Shawn said tightly, "and a bully, and it's a bad combination. And it's become a killing game."

"What do you mean?"

"If you want to hear news first, you should move your office to a saloon. A freighter came in afoot fifteen minutes ago. There was a slide on Cougar Mountain grade. Bill Fox's stage was wrecked. They'd dug the team out when this man started in. The passengers and mail are at Long Valley station. No one killed,'' she said, ''but it certainly wasn't for not trying.''

Callahan gazed out of the window. ''That's a steep grade. It could have been a slide.''

''It would be the first in six years. Do you think it would happen at the very moment the coach ran under an overhang? It was luck that no one was killed. But it won't be luck if the coaches don't run for a month.''

It came back to Callahan. Hoagland's rough threat—*Franchises aren't concrete . . . they can be broken.* A two-week holdup of mail and passengers would jeopardize the franchise. In post-office circles, slides were not considered a valid excuse.

Callahan moved about. He buckled on his gun belt. He poured water into the thick china basin. Shawn's hands took his shoulders and turned him.

''You could thank me,'' she said.

Callahan said soberly, ''I'm obliged. But you'd be better off to let me find things out for myself. Stanger will know about it.''

''I'd take the risk, Craig, if I thought it were worth it.''

She was a tender-lipped, provocative girl, obscurely exciting; and all Callahan could think of was Kitty Winans.

He stood at the mirror and ran a brush through his hair. He thought a moment before he told her:

''It isn't, Shawn. It was over before it started.''

When he looked around, she was at the door. ''I can't say you didn't warn me, can I?'' she said. ''But don't look for any more favors from me, Craig, because even flounces don't make a girl *that* much of a fool!''

5

CALLAHAN FOUND GENTRY IN A SHED ASSEMBLING picks, axes and shovels. In a black mood, Gentry said, "Man gets in the clear, and the next day a thousand dollars worth of rocks falls on him!"

"Going out tonight?"

"Not in Injun weather. I'll scrape up a road gang and we'll take off in the morning."

In the morning, workmen began to assemble in the stage yard to load pack-mules and crawl onto wagons. A sharp pleasure filled Callahan as he saddled his horse. He had been too long from the atmosphere of roadmaking—of heavy tools and hard-working men, and he looked forward to showing Gentry how fast a road could be made out of an avalanche.

The train strung out down the quiet dawn street of Reserve. A pack-train was just making up at the loading dock of a mountain freight outfit.

Four hours out, they broke for the nooning at the foot

of Cougar Mountain grade. Making the summit in a bare stand of lodge-pole, the road tipped down. The mountainside was steep, climbing by rims to blunt peaks still marbled with snow. A long, curving valley lay along the base of the mountains. Gentry pointed to the station, brown log boxes on the new-green of the spring grass. About a half-mile from here, they came upon the slide. It buried the road for a hundred yards, a flood of huge gray boulders, earth, and trees.

Leaving their ponies, they climbed across it. They found the dead team at the lower fringe of the slide. The coach had been removed, apparently still capable of being rolled, but the horses had been dropped and half-buried by the stones.

Gentry stood looking back up the slide. "How long?"

"Two weeks," Callahan decided.

"Then the mail's got to go around the other side, by pack train. Two weeks, without snow to alibi me, would break my franchise. I'd be washed up!"

Callahan took charge of setting up the camp. Because of the precipitous nature of the terrain, camp was made on the road itself. Messes were arranged and as the pup tents went up he started the first ragged gray stones rolling down the hillside.

That night they stayed at Long Valley Station. Another coach had come in. Twenty passengers now thronged the small station. Gentry told them:

"Anybody that's got to get to Reserve can go with the mail train. The rest will be better off to go back to Bitter Creek by stage tomorrow. We'll have things running again in two weeks."

A man said sourly, "And I passed up a chance to drum shoes in New York state, where they've got railroads!"

"Brother," Gentry snapped, "there's a power of folks came to Colorado just because there *ain't* any railroads!"

By the following night, the log-jam of derelict passengers was broken. By mule, a few went on to Reserve. By coach, the remainder returned to Bitter Creek. But on the meadow behind the station, freight trains began to pile up, dusty wagons hauling two or three trailers and pulled by five and six span of mules. Food, liquor and supplies for Reserve and the score of mountain communities it served began to mass like logs in a mill pond. Grain sacks ran empty and teams scoured on the washy spring grass. Teamsters broke into their loads for provisions.

A wagonmaster came to Gentry one morning with whiskey on his breath and sourness in his eyes.

"It's roads like yours," he declared, "that will be the death of freighting and staging. I've got three ton of vegetables from California, set down by U.P. at Bitter Creek. Better'n a thousand miles without spoilage. And now, by God, they set here under the sun and rot on a hundred-and-ten-mile haul!"

Gentry said, "Avalanches can happen to railroads, too. They can even happen to freighters that get too free with their advice."

Callahan left him alone those ten days of blasting and muscling at the slide. The old man was seeing the first tinge of death in the face of something he loved. He must know that a single slide after the railroad began competing—a single wagon-train of food spoiled—and he would be finished. His road would be forgotten by all but a few hapless passengers who failed to make the train. . . .

Gentry let the coaches roll again. A threadlike passage was driven through the granite. Two stages made it in, and one morning Hollis Lamerick and Kitty dismounted at the camp from the first stage from Reserve. Callahan, working near the upper margin of the slide, went to meet them.

Lamerick held an envelope in his hand and struck it against his leg. "Well, you were right. The governor of

Texas had the goodness to wire me that he'd pay fifty dollars for my partner's scalp, untanned; a hundred tanned. He says you're on the list, too.''

"And trying hard to get off." Callahan, dusty and sunburned, looked at Kitty. "If that's an apology in your eyes, forget it. I was taken too, once.''

The sun sparkled in the earrings she wore, and made her shade her eyes with her hand; her eyes were grave, and there was not the remnant of a smile on her mouth.

"You were right," she told him. "Hoagland *is* that kind—the kind to hold someone's arms while someone else gives the beating. And we were the ones he picked to do the beating. It was the bondholders he let us beat, and we thought we were doing them a service.''

Lamerick growled, "Kathleen, you're getting ahead of things. We don't *know* that he isn't building a substantial railroad this time. It's possible he's realized there was more money in hauling freight and passengers than in what he did in Texas.''

Callahan smiled. "That was the best business in the world. Half of every bond we sold he sent away, banked it out-of-state. He sold his railroad land as fast as he could claim it. He must have put away a hundred thousand. And I'll cover all bets that he hasn't sunk more than ten thousand in this road.''

Lamerick's face resisted it. "I've looked at the road, myself. I see no difference between our road and the U.P., except that we're narrow-gage. No difference.''

"And a Piute," said Callahan, "wouldn't see much difference between a bottle of vinegar and a bottle of whiskey, until he'd tried them. Lamerick, this road isn't ballasted, it's dusted with gravel! It doesn't bridge, it toe-dances on two-by-fours! I could bend the rails with my hands, and the ties—they're doing their seasoning right in the ground. They'll start shrinking before long and you'll have seven different gages of track. I went over every yard of it, afoot, before I jumped into this. I know what he's doing. And I know how to lick him.''

"When you say, 'lick him,' " Lamerick drily pointed out, "you're saying, 'lick Reserve.' Including myself, and Sizemore, and Judge Lightfoot, and a few hundred investors. The noose is big, Callahan. You can't hang him without hanging us."

A jay swooped past; a muleskinner whacked his team along with a rock-sled combing dust behind. The stage team minced into the narrow cut through the slide.

Lamerick raised a hand to the driver. "Kathleen, go along to the station. We'll go back on the evening stage."

She shook her head, smiling. "Not until I hear what *this* railroader is selling."

They walked up the road, out of the dust and litter of the camp. Through the steeple tops of the pines, five miles east, Callahan could see a white feather of dust where a railroad grading crew was blasting. The sound came moments later, like a faint rumble of mountain thunder.

"If it weren't for you and the rest," Callahan said, "I'd be over there on the railroad with a hired crew of roughnecks, tearing up track. I could do it, legally. I've got the cease and desist, and I guess you could say I served it the other night. I'd make guerrilla warfare, if I had to. Every time he went forward by one bridge, I'd burn another. But I wanted to work out something that would take care of everybody. Getting down to cases," he said, "how much of the voting stock do you hold?"

"A third. I put up two-thirds of the cash to start, he put up a third and the location stakes."

"With enough proxies, you could out-vote him, couldn't you?"

"If you're talking about a vote to discontinue the project, I don't expect to find many men willing to give me their proxies."

"I'm talking about reorganizing. Vote yourself chief of construction, with me as your assistant. And take care of Roy Gentry by giving him a few hundred shares for his franchise. Then we'll see about building a railroad.''

''And yet,'' Lamerick frowned, ''I have the feeling that Hoagland's still got a hole-card somewhere.''

''Play yours, then,'' Callahan said impatiently. ''I've shown you the way. If you want to string along with him until the investors begin talking about you and him in the same breath—''

''Craig's right,'' Kitty said. ''If you don't fight him with votes now, you may have to fight with guns later.''

There was a sharp, concussive powder-blast at a distance. Callahan glanced down the grade. He had not authorized a shot. But he did not see the dust, and a moment later as the echoes poured back from the hills he heard a patter of small stones. There was a frozen moment of standing there, listening and searching, and then Kitty's sharp question:

''Craig, are they blasting above us?''

He looked up the rough staircase of rimrock ledges mounting to the peaks. He had the curious sensation that something was out of plumb. A gray-green island of pines two hundred feet above seemed to be leaning toward them. Then he saw a giant block of granite separate itself from a buttress, like a keystone, and go into a slow fall toward the road.

The moment shattered. He was sweeping Kitty up in his arms and lunging toward the slide. He heard his own voice bawling something. Down the road, workmen looked around, resting on their shovels. Then they, too, began to run deeper into the slide.

A fragment of a rim high above the road had torn loose. Powdersmoke drifted through the trees and boulders were bounding down the steep hillside in a tawny fog.

Lamerick was there, trying to take Kitty from him. He shouted something in his face and swerved from him. There was a patter of small stones and then an impact that trembled in the earth. Bounding away, the boulder struck a mule tied to a tree and carried it overside. Ahead of Callahan, dust blossomed in small spurts from the road. A sharp pain struck his foot and he fell with the girl.

Callahan put her over his shoulder in a rude fireman's carry. Her hands clutched him as he ran on. Stones were landing in the old slide. A skinner deserted his team and in panic dived over the edge. Picks and shovels blocked the narrow cut.

Then, with a grinding roar, the main body of the blast struck the grade. It was a blunt, concussive sound, and then a grating rattle of tons of disturbed granite jarring across the roadbed. Another stone ricocheted into Callahan's back. Again he tripped, and this time he crawled against a boulder near the bank and crouched there above the girl.

After a long time the surf-like roaring ebbed; it was a dusty silence struck with the occasional crumpling descent of a single stone down the hill. Then it was over.

Callahan sat back. Up the grade, the old slide merged into a new one. Dust drifted over the rubble. Half-buried, a mule could be seen raising and lowering its head. A pine lay, roots-up, across the road.

Craig looked at Kitty. She was gray with dust, her bonnet hung by the ribbons and her dark hair had come loose.

He helped her up. "I've put it off too long," he said. "I'm going to do it."

"Do what?"

He framed her face with his hands and kissed her on the mouth. "What I've told myself I'd do sooner or later. It took a slide to make me realize some things can't wait. You get killed, and there you are—the most important things left undone."

She drew away, her expression arch. "I'm not sure this is the time and place to do it, however."

"Or that I'm the one to do it?"

"That remains to be seen, too," Kitty said. "You've got plenty of time before the next excitement, I hope."

"That's what I'm not sure of," Callahan sighed.

Lamerick's face was beginning to color. "What kind of gang are you running, Callahan? I thought you were the one who knew all about ramrodding a road-gang!"

Callahan pushed by him, heading for the horse-corral. Gentry was coming from somewhere, shirtless and roaring. "Who in the tarnal hell—!"

Callahan said, "No loss, Roy. Just a couple of mules and two weeks' work. You're a peaceable man, so I won't ask you along on this ride I'm taking."

Gentry, his chest working, stared upward. "It was a shot, wasn't it?"

The line of saddle-horses was restive. Callahan tightened cinches, and was about to mount when Gentry caught out his horse and swung up. "I'm a patient man," he said, "but I'm not yellow."

They were wheeling toward the camp when Hollis Lamerick strode in.

"There won't be a better time to reorganize this outfit than now," he said.

"Can you spare me a horse?"

Near Cougar Mountain summit, a trail split east, sloughing from the mountain into the rough foothills where the railroad was building. Lamerick turned his pony down this trail. As Callahan followed, Gentry shook his head.

"He'd be up on the rims."

"Not unless he's crazy. He'd have cut a half-hour fuse and taken off for wherever he'd come from . . . probably the railroad camp."

After a moment, Gentry grunted and came along.

They worked slowly eastward against a cool breeze off the mountains. The growth was scent, of tough mountain shrubs and grasses and patches of squaw-carpet. Hillsides fell off into the canyons, canyons led them along streams still brown with the thaw, and then they would strike a switchbacking ascent to a ridge a little higher than the last. On one of these, with the wind cold and stiff in his face, Callahan studied the brown scar of the railroad coming across the apron of the Rockies and stalling against the hip of a mountain. Disapproval touched his face: There was no reason for a tunnel there. An easy swing westward, a trestle across a narrow canyon, and the road would have been three miles closer to Reserve by now.

His carbine rested across the fork of the saddle. Craig's fingers pressed around the loading lever in sudden reaction. There was movement on a hillside southeast of them. He spoke to Lamerick. "Better if you go in first. If we show up, there'll be trouble right off."

"I don't think Hoagland would be out here anyway. He was in town when I left."

"Go on," Callahan commanded shortly. "Lay it down to Braga and whoever's around. Fire everybody in sight, but let them know there'll be more work after the smoke clears to hell out of here."

After he was out of earshot, Callahan turned to Gentry. "See him?"

"Ten minutes ago. We're coming to a meeting with him, if he don't see us first."

A horse worked in and out of mottes of leafless aspen a mile away. To gain the railroad camp, the rider would have to swing around the toe of the same bony ridge through which the road was tunneling. Lamerick would pass ahead of the rider, having a lead on him, but his town-eyes would not be likely to discover him.

Callahan waited five minutes. Then he rode ahead.

From another lift of timber they watched Lamerick ride from a screen of pines into the clutter of the construction camp. Workmen drifted along the grade. There was no sign of the other horseman. Callahan's nerves began to vibrate. He brought a shell under the firing pin and let the pony take the downslope at a fast jog.

They came into a small wallow where a creek ran through greenish boulders. Above them, the stream fell whitely down a steep and narrow canyon, and it was from this canyon that the horseman must come to reach the camp.

They drifted to within a hundred yards of the side-trail, hidden in gray service-berry. Ten minutes passed. A hawk wheeled above them. There were sounds from the camp a half mile away—the ring of metal and the slow scrape of shovels. A supply train chuffed in.

Callahan's pony turned its head to gaze up-canyon. A moment later a roan horse flecked with lather pushed dispiritedly into view. The rider was a compact-looking man in a gray work-shirt. He held a browned carbine in his right hand, watching the trail closely as he rode. Welts striped the flank of the horse where a small-roweled spur had raked it. He could have been any rail-road worker coming in from hunting meat or locating stakes; but the horse carried saddlebags too large for ammunition and too small for transit and claim. They looked to Callahan about right for dynamite and fuse.

He raised the carbine; the horseman twisted suddenly in the saddle and saw him, and Callahan saw the man's gun swing and had a darting glimpse of a brown, flat face before the gun crashed.

Earth exploded between him and Gentry. A slug screamed away. Callahan's horse went crazy. It began pitching toward the creek as he clubbed it over the head with his gun. He could hear Gentry yelling at his horse, and there was a hard rattle of gravel from the trail. He turned and saw the roan horse buck-jumping uphill into the trees. He fired a shot over the man's head and shouted at him.

Gentry had his horse under control. He shouted at Craig, "Cut him off from the camp! I'll take the trail . . ."

Slashing into the pines, Callahan took the hill, driv-ing on a tangent between the trail and the camp. The

pines were an island on the stony mountainside, which
ascended steeply to timberline. A horseman could be
flushed from cover in an hour's time. We've got him,
he thought; but having a tiger in a sack did not amount
to capture. The man in there did not know but what he
was being sought for murder. He would not walk out
with his hands up.

It was suddenly quiet. Callahan reined in. Sounds
from the railroad camp had ceased, except for a few
voices quizzically raised. Then there was a rattle of
hoofs and he put the pony forward. The hoof-sounds
halted. Callahan's hand brought the horse in sharply.
Through the trees he could see what was beyond the
growth: A long dike of granite lying across the slope
like an arm. There would be no riding a horse across it
to a higher trail. It would be south, to the trail; or north,
to the camp, and capture.

Callahan left the horse and walked quietly through
the pine needles. There was the fragrance of pitch and
the sound of his own tight breathing. After a while he
heard a horse moving, and he pressed against a tree
and waited . . . The roan pony came into view; he had
a sick instant of trying to keep himself from firing at it
instead of the rider. But as it came forward through the
service-berry, he saw that it was riderless: The reins
had been tied to the horn.

Callahan began to run. He slanted through the trees
toward open ground. He could hear a man moving:
Branches cracked and once it seemed that he had fallen.
Then it was silent again. Craig slowed. He was walking
carefully down an aisle of cinnamon-barked pines when
he heard footfalls, not in pine-needles but on stone.

He came out the back door of the trees and saw the
man sliding into a deep groove in the granite: It appeared as though the stone had been sliced and the
wedge removed like a center-slice of bread. A man
could just squeeze himself in there like a wounded fox
and wait . . .

The carbine slammed again. Callahan dropped. Sighting, he could not see the gunman. He backed into the trees and began to run. The slot was a transverse one; from farther south, it provided no shelter at all. He had a view of clothing and gunmetal. The rifle roared again and bark flew ten feet ahead of him. Callahan hit the ground.

Then he took his time. The man in the slot was perfectly visible. He himself was screened by brush. He reached a tree and made sure he had a shell in the chamber. He chanced a long look. The gunman was trying to climb. Where the fissure squeezed in, it was possible to scramble higher, making it to the next step of rimrock.

Callahan shouted, "Dead or alive, mister!"

The fugitive writhed and the carbine came to his shoulder; but Callahan's gun had driven its yellow flame out and the echoes of it slammed back with force that made him wince.

The gun rattled down the rocks. The man began to fall, but caught halfway down and hung there, head down. Callahan could see blood dripping from the tip of his nose. He slowly lowered the gun. He shook his head, as though he had been clipped on the chin. Then he got up and went back to his horse.

Only Tom Braga was at the camp. Several score workmen, some of them Chinese, some Irish immigrants, were distributing ballast while miners sledged star-drills in the tunnel. A weathered colony of tents sheltered the Chinese; a shabby camp train on a siding housed the white workers. On slender poles, a thread of new copper wire dipped northward toward Bitter Creek.

Hollis Lamerick was with Braga at the superintendent's yellow car, ahead of the clerical car and store. A cluster of office workers stood at the steps of the clerical car. Braga, short and surly, a long bandage across his forehead, stood by the tracks with his arms folded. His face was still puffy with bruises, but Callahan could look into the thorny eyes and think,

I licked everything out of him but the fight. Nobody will ever do that.

Lamerick looked at Callahan and Gentry. He and Braga had been arguing: Rancor was in both their faces.

Lamerick asked quickly: "What was the firing?"

"We dropped him. He wouldn't surrender. What was the pay, Tom?" he asked Braga. "Hunter's wages?"

Braga spat. "You get crazier all the time."

". . . Why wrangle over it? We'll find his name in his clothes and on the payroll. That's all the proof I want to clear my conscience. How would you clear yours, if anyone had been killed?"

Suddenly Lamerick said, "Pack your duffle and get out. If you want to argue, argue with Hoagland."

Braga regarded him steadily. "What gets into a fellow to go to war against himself?" He went off to a camp car and presently returned with a brown carpetbag and a coat slung over his shoulder. "I'll check out a horse," he said drily. He walked on to the corral.

Lamerick went to the clerical car. "Draw your time at the office in Reserve," he told the clerks. "We'll be hiring again in a week or two."

In the deserted car with its dusty letter-presses and ledgers, he went to work, abstracting everything he needed to block Hoagland from a coup. He inspected the safe. There were only a few hundred dollars on hand.

"We keep the cash in town," he told Craig. "At least I know that much. There's thirty thousand gold in the safe."

"Or was," Callahan said.

Lamerick looked at him, cleared his throat and briskly locked the safe. "We'd better go on. It will be dark before we make it."

They followed the stakes in. The trail following the locations stakes was rough and roundabout. It cut into the high foothills and drifted out again. Finally it sloped into an easy grade a mile short of Reserve. Dusk was over the mountain town like smoke as they rode in. Lights were coming up behind dusty panes, mothers screeched after children and a crew of miners trudged in from one of the closer hardrock mines.''

Lamerick looked exhausted. ''I'll go to my hotel. Be at the office after dinner.''

Callahan and Gentry returned to the stage station to sluice off trail dirt. After heating water, Gentry began to scrape with a razor. It came to Craig, then, that he had hardly spoken since they flushed the dynamiter. The silence began to disturb him.

''You aren't going to Injun on us, are you?'' he asked.

Gentry flicked peppery lather at the wood-box. ''I reckon that second slide knocked the stretch out of me. Up to then, you couldn't have given me a railroad. I've put thirty years into proving that any place you could take a horse, you could take a Concord. But all of a sudden it don't matter much whether you can or not. Nobody gives a damn, if there's a smoke-belchin' monster to ride, instead.''

Callahan smiled. ''That's me talking, Roy, thirty years from now. Somebody will come along with a transcontinental line of balloons and you'll have to give people ether to get them onto a train. But when it happens, I hope somebody trades me balloon stock for railroad stock.''

Gentry finished and flipped back the lid of the coffee pot. He said wearily, ''And when they do, you'd give the whole kit and bilin' away if you could go back to Colorado and build your first railroad again. That's the way of us, Callahan.''

6

At eight o'clock they walked up the street to the railroad office. Chips of lamplight escaped through the green blinds. A blunt murmur of voices came through the door. Sizemore, the banker, let them in. He punished a cigar as he stood aside. He was coatless and had loosened his tie. Behind the partition, a large maptable held an untidy exhibit of ledgers, papers and fuming saucers serving as ash-trays. Judge Cady Lightfoot, ominous patriarch of the group, sat at one end of the table with a whiskey bottle at his elbow. His deep-socketed eyes followed the men as they came in.

Leaning against a partition, Marsh Hoagland scratched a match for a half-smoked cigar. His face was sober and deeply-cut with lines, locked in a frown. Through the smoke he regarded Callahan, with slow concentration. Then heavy features were dour, but there was no panic in them, and Callahan recalled one of the first things he had learned about the man—that his deceptiveness and sureness increased as the pressure was put on him.

Judge Lightfoot, in his massive baritone, said, "Sit down. Court will come to order."

Callahan took a chair and Sizemore wordlessly offered a cigar. Looking out-of-place, Gentry sat beside Lamerick, but Hoagland stayed on his feet.

"As I understand it," Lightfoot said, "we thought this man was building a railroad, and it turns out we've got something an amusement park wouldn't own up to. What are we going to do about it?"

"I could tell you," Callahan said, "but I don't expect anybody would want to pull the trigger."

Hoagland drew on the cigar and said nothing.

"The first thing," Sizemore said, "is to vote in a new chief engineer. But we can't do that until tomorrow. We don't have enough votes among us. Hoagland," he said sourly, "maybe you could suggest something."

Hoagland stirred. "Yes. If you want a suggestion."

They waited, not looking at him. But Callahan studied him in a kind of fascination.

Hoagland supported his weight on his elbows, turning the cigar slowly between his fingers. "Would it be asking too much for you to get information from the association of railroads before you fire me?"

"What's that?" Callahan asked. "A club for down-and-out brakemen? I never heard of it."

Lamerick's face had eased. He avoided Callahan's eyes. He said, "I suppose it doesn't have to be decided tonight. Lightfoot, can you draft us a letter to this—whatever it is—and send it under you official seal?"

Callahan was on his feet, staring down at them. "By God, if you old women want to let him tie a can to your tails, why should I worry?"

Sizemore's brows pulled. "What you don't seem to see, Callahan, is that the whole town may stand or fall by what happens to us!"

"I see that!" Callahan snapped.

From the door, Gentry's voice came in puzzled alarm. "What the hell!"

Chairs scraped back. Callahan went out onto the walk beside him. A line of saddle- and pack-horses was breaking up before Emory's Livery Stable. Callahan recognized Captain Stanger's rawhide form swinging out of saddle.

Gentry was whispering. "By God, boys! It had to come. That boarding-house general wa'n't fit to lead an old soldiers' parade!"

Lamerick padlocked the office and they went down. Miners were stringing out of the saloons and cafes. There were six men with Stanger. His tunic was blood-stained. He had lost his hat. One of the other men suddenly grasped at his saddle-horn but missed it and went overside. Two men caught him and laid him on the ground.

The other horses were laden with the remnants of equipment. Stanger looked at the crowd like a man being persecuted. "Utes!" he said. "They attacked in force at Crow Creek. We'd tracked them—same gang that scalped the wood-cutters."

"Where's the rest?" someone asked.

Stanger's jaw was loose. He bent his head and wiped his forehead with his sleeve. "Massacred," he said. "Security guard failed us. They hit at dawn. We were lucky, that's all—"

"But the other eight," Gentry said softly, "weren't."

Stanger's head turned. "Is that my fault? Damn it, man, is it my fault if a guard slept?"

A lean trooper gripped his pommel with both hands. "Captain, that ain't so. Corporal Ensley had orders to—"

Stanger turned his horse into the stable. "That will be decided," he said . . .

When Craig and Gentry left the crowd, Hoagland had gone. Lamerick tried to fumble an explanation but Callahan pushed past him and went back to the stage depot.

Sitting over coffee, Callahan told Gentry: "If he'd

pulled out a bottle of snakebite cure, they'd have fought each other to buy it. All they want is to be fair. That takes time. And all he wants is time. They'll paper their walls with those bonds next fall—the damned fools!''

"In fact,'' Gentry said, "the only thing you like about Hollis Lamerick is his daughter.''

After a while Hollis Lamerick came, smelling of the barbershop. He bore an envelope addressed to the telegraph agent at Bitter Creek. His face craved understanding as he gave Gentry the letter.

"Send this with the mail train,'' he said. "You can see our position. If it turns out he *is* right about the line being adequate for mountain freight—''

"Go to hell,'' said Callahan.

He went into the yard. A hostler was watering stock. Gentry came out to fork up hay, and at eleven Shawn Miller came to the station with a straw suitcase in her hand.

"Where's the stage?'' she asked Callahan.

Callahan gave it back to her for the other day. "Maybe you'd better move to the stage office and keep up with things. There was another slide. Act of God. No stage, Shawn. Not for two weeks.''

There was bluish skin under her eyes, and her face was drawn. "Craig, I've got to get away! This town's going crazy!''

"Most of them seem to like it that way.''

"Don't joke!'' she said. "It was bad enough to see you beaten, and Braga whipped, and hear men planning to burn the stage depot if you didn't stop interfering with the railroad. But when they start to have public whippings!''

At once he knew; but he asked shortly: "Who's whipping who?''

"Stanger . . . He's whipping Ensley, the trooper who's supposed to have caused the massacre. Hoagland was talking him into it last night. He tried him this morning, with himself as judge advocate and defense counsel! They'll whip him in front of Emory's at noon. I don't want to be here, Craig! I can't stay in town and hear it.''

She grasped only the surface brutality, but what he saw was the savage terror of a commander who had let eight of his men be slaughtered . . . a numbed seeking after exoneration for himself by throwing the blame on another.

Callahan got his Stetson and told Gentry, ''I'm going down to watch the whipping. Trooper Ensley's to be hided in front of Emory's. Better spruce up and come down.''

There was a narrow aisle down the middle of the street before the livery stable: Men jammed the boardwalks and the street itself. There was much subdued talk, an occasional shame-faced chuckle. He discovered Lamerick and Sizemore back in the margin of onlookers.

There was a reluctant pressing-back. Callahan wedged forward and standing in the front rank got his shoulder against the wall of the building. A timber thrust out above the hayloft door, like a hang-tree. A man standing on baled hay tossed out the hay-hook and another handler let the rope down through the block.

Captain Stanger appeared. A civilian prodded Corporal Ensley through the door. The man's hands were tied before him and he was bare-headed and sallow.

The crowd went silent. Stanger cleared his throat and unfolded a paper. His hands trembled. His voice clogged as he began to read:

''. . . that you shall receive one hundred lashes, and be drummed out of the service.'' Stanger finished reading. He snapped to attention and said something to the man who had brought the trooper out.

Ensley began to struggle, suddenly, shouting curses at the captain. But a gang of men surrounded him and the rope binding his hands was caught by the hay-hook. They hauled him to his toes. Stanger held a long, supple whip about the fatness and length of a mature king-snake.

''Will you count?'' Stanger asked the hostler. Stark cruelty was in his eyes.

The man nodded. Without warning Stanger's shoulder rolled and the whip went out. Ensley writhed, but did not cry out.

''One!'' the hostler continued.

Stanger struck again. His face was turning red. He kept moistening his lips. He struck four times, moving about as Ensley's body turned on the twist of the rope. The corporal's shirt was torn; blood began to stream. Now his back was to Callahan; the whip popped near him as it recoiled.

He looked up again, his mouth hardening. As Stanger threw the whip back, Callahan caught it. He yanked. It was out of the cavalryman's hand.

''You crazy fool!'' Stanger shouted.

Callahan moved forward and got his back to the wall. ''You don't savvy,'' he told Stanger. ''They just want to see someone whipped. They don't care particularly who. In fact, I think they'll find this an improvement.''

He drove the whip at Stanger's face. It struck in a hard coil of plaited leather, smashing his lips and cutting his eye. He went to his knees in agony. In an instant he was struggling up, pulling at his Colt. Callahan slashed at the man's arm. He caught it and yanked; as Stanger stumbled close he struck him across the nose with the butt of the blacksnake. Stanger fell aside, blinded, and Callahan threw his gun in the dirt.

No one moved. Ensley swung on the long rope. The men were utterly quiet. Callahan's boots never stirred, but his upper body pivoted and his shoulder dipped, time after time, without weariness and without pity. Stanger floundered against the door of the stable, half-rising, falling again, turning his face to the planks and again facing outward and crying in pain and rage.

Sweat pitted Callahan's face. He was aware of the miracle of the crowd, and knew at last why it was—they were not many men, but one man controllable because they had no stake whatever in this. He had been right: A proxy would do as well as the proper victim.

He cut with the whip until the rage went out of Stanger's voice. He watched the captain fall to the boardwalk and crawl toward the legs of the men ringing him in, hunting shelter. He threw the whip down, then, walking to where the rope was tied which held the corporal up, he cut it loose. He gave the man a dollar.

"Buy yourself a couple," he said.

No one attempted to stop him as he departed.

He was in the National for an hour, drinking and lackadaisically betting on roulette and watching the dice tumble in the chuckaluck cages. He was out eighty-five dollars when Roy Gentry found him. Gentry made a couple of bets on roulette, sitting beside Callahan, but he did not speak. Craig could almost hear a wire of nervousness vibrating in him.

Finally Gentry grunted: "Do we have to do this?"

Callahan shrugged and followed him to the bar. A shirt-sleeved barman brought them steam beer, slicing the suds neatly with an ivory knife. Gentry salted his beer and sipped it.

"You and the devil must have cooed in the same bassinette," he growled.

"Stanger's been begging for it. Nobody seemed to think he was being mistreated."

Gentry mused. "Funny thing—Hoagland took off during the show."

"Why shouldn't he? He's got a railroad to build. He's got to be out buying rusty rails and green ties."

"Well, he's heeled for the job. He took everything in the safe and disappeared. Thirty thousand—gold. Lamerick and Sizemore are crazy, but they were ashamed to come after you. So I came."

Callahan's jaw muscles loosened, and Gentry grinned. "You look interested, after all. The reason I figger Stanger got swindled is that Hoagland ribbed him up to the whipping to bunch everybody in town down here." He finished his beer in four gulping swallows. "Why don't we go back to the station, where we can talk?"

In the cold back office of the stage depot, Lamerick

sat with a cigar in his mouth and the sickest face Callahan had ever seen. Callahan breathed deeply. Down through the blood vessels and nerves of his body, he could feel warmth trickling. But he gave the man a lofty scowl and wrestled the tip from a cigar with his teeth.

Lamerick said, "I won't make any more of an ass of myself by apologizing."

"I don't know as you could."

Lamerick's pained face turned up. "Where could he go, Craig?"

"How should I know?"

"But you know him better than we do! My God! I sat in that office all night, with a shotgun, just in case— And I had a man in the place this morning, too. Then we all went down to see the whipping."

He slowly pounded his knees with his palms. "And then I went back. He'd taken all the cash—gold and yellowbacks! And burned the papers. . . . Where the hell would he go?" he pleaded.

Callahan gazed out the window. "Why ask me? I'm a stage man. Last night my pardner and I tried to be railroad men. You put the big britches on us. I'm going to get some rest," he told Gentry.

He gripped the cold white knob, but the railroad man strode after him. "Listen, Callahan! It was reasonable enough, what he said. But I didn't entirely believe him, that's why I guarded the office. I wanted to be sure. We'll listen to you, now. I talked to Lightfoot and Sizemore, and they'll back you for superintendent. But without that money, we're shipped! We're already overextended."

Callahan considered . . . "The way he worked before, he had bank deposits all over the state of Kansas. I saw a batch of passbooks in his desk once. Now, if you could find the passbooks, you'd be able to track him down, sooner or later. Maybe."

"Yes, but what about taking after him now? It's only been two or three hours."

"That's a long time, as fast as he moves."

He opened the door, and Lamerick was silent, his eyes bitter. Callahan hesitated.

"Will you put that all in writing?"

Lamerick had a paper in his pocket. "Done!"

Callahan looked at it. He began to rub his hands. "Roy, get a horse out. Fastest thing in the yard."

Lamerick trailed him as he paced into his bedroom. "You can only ride one direction at once. God knows where he's gone."

"But a good bet would be he went back to end-of-track. He'd probably go by the route they've staked out. He wouldn't want to show himself in our camp, and he'd have to, to get by it. I'd expect him to have the rest of his cash hidden around the railroad, probably in his bunk or office."

"That's a lot of guessing," Lamerick said dubiously.

"Yes. But don't forget railroads are faster than horses, and once he makes it there he can beat us into Bitter Creek by six hours." He stood there with his carbine in his hands, a smile faintly turning his lips. "It's been a long pull, Lamerick. But I've finally got him on the short end of the rope."

Gentry had saddled one horse and was throwing a blanket on another when Callahan ran out with a booted gun and some food rolled in a blanket. Tying it behind the cantle, he told Gentry hurriedly, "I'm going like hell, Roy. I'm picking off the best plug at each station, but if you want to try to keep up—"

"You're following the stage road then?"

"How else? He'll be halfway back to the camp by that goatpath he's charted. But the stage road is a short-cut to the Bridge Creek crossing."

"That's twenty miles beyond the slide!" Gentry's face began to burn. "Listen! You want to get there first and be waitin' on him?"

"All I ask is a chance to dive at the caboose."

"Then, by God, what you want is a stagecoach! Stagecoach will outrun a hoss any time. Hosses to Long

Valley . . . stagecoach from there. And by God I'll drive her myself!''

Callahan swung up, grinning. "Stage outrun a horse?''

"You think it won't? It'll damn well outrun a coal-burner this trip.''

There was only one relay between Reserve and the slide. They abandoned their blown horses here and took off on new mounts. Callahan's eye measured the sun as they slanted up the side of Cougar Mountain. Darkness would whip them, for at night a stage, or even a horse, could not make the time that a locomotive could. It would be a race with sundown.

They descended a vague deer-train to avoid the slide. Following a deep canyon, they came out in mid-afternoon on the green apron of Long Valley. From the foothills, they could see the stage station, a derelict city of stranded freight outfits.

Gentry began to stew. "If that mail coach ain't come down today, they'll be fur flyin'!''

As they loped in, they saw the dusty olive green coach in the yard, its tongue resting on the ground. Gentry's heels thumped to the ground. "Hitch 'em!" he bawled. "Give me a team, damn it!''

Hostlers began to assemble. The station keeper stood on the porch and argued with him.

"Roy, it ain't begun to be cleared! You couldn't take a dogsled over that-there slide.''

"Ain't going that direction!''

Gentry rawhided the hostlers into the corral and took charge of the cutting-out. Callahan stood in the yard and looked for someone, and presently she came to the door. Seeing him, her face gladdened. Callahan caught her by the waist.

"Craig, what's happened? I've been out of my head, waiting—We heard a man was killed at the railroad camp, but nobody seemed to know who.''

Callahan smiled. "It's been a quiet week-end," he

said. "Not much doing at all. But they took a vote this morning and decided to let me build the road instead of Marsh Hoagland. We're tying to catch Hoagland now to tell him."

"That's only part of it," she said suspiciously. "What's the rest?"

"The rest is he's got all the company cash with him. There won't be a road if we don't stop him. So what I was going to say to you will have to wait till I get back."

She gathered up her skirts with a quick motion and half-turned. "I'm going along."

Callahan turned her back. "You're staying here. Coaches turn over. Utes light fires in roads." He saw Gentry and the hostlers backing the team onto the pole. "If you want to help, just pray that for once a stage-coach outruns a train."

From the station house, the agent ran with a long-barreled rifle and a coat over his arm. Gentry waved him back. "Can't take you, Harry! These nags are going to need every break we can give them."

"You can't stop a train!" Kitty told Craig. "What will you do—flag him down? Light a flare?"

"That's what I'll be thinking about between here and Bridge Creek," he told her. "And something else I'll be thinking about is this—"

It was less hurried than the other day, lingering with a poignant sweetness. Her body was supple and strong against him, and he felt her fingers holding him, and then he heard the coach-tires grind back and forth and knew the team was ready. But she held him an instant longer, whispering:

"If I had to choose between you and the railroad, you know which it would be. So if you're in doubt about anything, think about me."

"Even when I'm not in doubt," Craig said.

Gentry was shouting at him as he bulled the team around toward the road. He held it long enough for him to put a foot on the hub and swing up. The stage ground out of the yard and onto the road spearing across the valley into the hills.

After a while Callahan realized the sun was full on the side of his face. It was deep in the west. On the rises, he searched for train-smoke in the broken hills beyond the sage. He sat there with his coat collar turned up and one hand gripping the cold iron rail, praying to and scorning the gods of staging whom Gentry worshipped. The road was winding lunacy—hugging the land as though terrified of being separated from it for an instant. A gully would knock the bottom out of the road, the horses would stream through it and the Concord would hit bedrock with a lunge. Then rocks would rise from the range before them and they would twist and dodge like an old cow in a brush pasture.

Once Gentry precipitately tromped the brake and handed the team in. Doggedly staring ahead, he said, "Even a hoss is only human. Got to rest 'em."

"How far to the relay?"

"Three mile. Then Bridge Creek. Another four, say."

A feather of sound drifted down-wind. Their eyes touched brittlely. "That's it!" said Callahan. "He's got his steam."

"How much time can he make?"

"On those rails, cream would sour in ten minutes. Not over twenty-five or thirty miles an hour."

Gentry seemed to sag. "Twenty-five!"

He had never, Callahan knew, travelled faster than fifteen, and that with a fast team on a good road. It was a sad end for a proud stage man, racing a work-engine on jerry-laid rails, and making less than half its time . . .

"Well, damn, we ain't going to beat his time a-settin' here!" said Gentry. He kicked the brake off the notch.

They bucked through a narrow pass where sage scratched the panels and crackled under the wheels, and a few minutes later Gentry ordered, "Grub out that horn in the boot and blow your lungs out."

Raising the battered bugle from under the seat, Callahan blew a squawking call. When they smoked into the stage-yard a few moments later, the team was already half-hitched. This was a small, one-man swing station, and Callahan helped with the horses. As Gentry ascended the box, he drew both carbines from the boots and cocked them. Sitting there, then, he heard a distant stutter of steam-valves. The station keeper grinned up at them, not understanding.

"Watch out for trains, Roy! You and that work-train are about to run a dead-heat to the crossin'!"

The stage rattled out of the yard. They were on a tilted prairie of lavender sage. In a clear amber sky, the sun was sagging behind the hills. Darkness would come swiftly, but it was only another fifteen minutes to the crossing, now.

Gentry's arms extended straight out over the dusty, clattering void between foot-board and horses. He had freed the horses: They were in a runaway. Dust boiled around them and smoked in their passage. Callahan tried to recall the ex-plan of the crossing.

Bridge Creek was a sandy, shallow stream in a gully only twenty feet deep, screened with sage and an occasional grove of aspen. A hundred feet south of the stream, the stage-road crossed the tracks before jumping the gully on a short trestle. He thought of all the ways to stop a train: Burn the bridge—no time for that. Dynamite it—no dynamite. Block the tracks . . .

Gentry was weighing the same thing. "Train got any vital parts, like other pests?" he asked.

"Just the engineer, and engineers can duck or be missed!"

"Then we got to block the road. He'd be hell-and-gone ahead of us by the time we made Bitter Creek. He'd be on the night mail and headin' for California."

"What would we block it with?"

Callahan already knew. But he would not be the man

to suggest it. Gentry knew, too. He spat and shook his head, and would not voice it. They lunged on.

The noise of the train was a steady pound, now. A horse turned its head to stare toward the foothills. They came up onto a plateau and saw the crossing a quarter-mile ahead of them. Rails gleamed on a spindly trestle. Bridge Creek was traceable only by its sentinel trees. Callahan looked for rocks—not too large, not too small. He looked for logs. And he knew even then that there was only one way to do it.

Gentry was bringing the bits into the wheelers' mouths, then into the swings', the leaders'. He had the horses in the breeching, fighting against him. They were coming into a tossing trot as they approached the tracks in their ruts of tired planks.

"Ready?" Gentry yelled. He looked around to measure; the train was perfectly visible, black and ugly, with spark-flecked smoke streaming on its own wind as it curved through the sagebrush toward them.

"Ready for what?" Callahan shouted.

"To unhitch 'em! Unlatch the tugs on your side. Then git!"

Right to the last, the team resisted him, as if their own instinct was against the sacrilege. They danced across the tracks and he stopped them six feet beyond, the rails passing between the fore and rear wheels. He stood on the long brake-lever to set them, and then jumped down, lugging his carbine.

Callahan's knife slashed the tugs free. He heard Gentry swearing as he undid the snaps. Gentry said, "God forgive me!" and fell back into the brush. The team bolted. Callahan felt the hammer of drivers in the earth. He heard the brakes go on with a scream. Then there was a crack of rifle-fire and he fell in the brush and lay quiet, watching for the coming move.

With brakes full on, the locomotive, pulling a single car—Hoagland's office—struck the stage. An incredible noise arose; an astonishing amount of junk flew. A wheel was bounding through the brush. Wood, leather, canvas, metal, filled the air. But the tough body of the coach was rolling and slewing along before the train, onto the bridge.

Something happened to the engine's dolly. It was on the ties, thumping with wild rhythm. The train tilted, recovered, and then the blunt cow-catcher dug into the ties of the bridge and began to plow . . .

Callahan, running forward, saw the red office-car fall twenty feet and land in the stream. The locomotive stopped crosswise on the bridge; it did not fall.

Callahan fell behind a stump near the bank. He could see the broken car, its windows shattered and its trucks flung aside. There was no indication of life in it, and he peered at the engine. A head came over the sill of a window. He fired, and heard Gentry's .44 carbine below. The face was that of Tom Braga, his bandage still showing. Braga sank back. The slugs tore at the wooden tongue-and-groove siding beneath the window. They chewed it to white splinters, and Braga rose up with blood on him and tried to lean on the sill by one hand, raising a revolver with the other. But the gun dropped into the creek. He fell against the side of the cab and twisted, and finally fell down the steps and onto the trestle.

There was life in the office car, suddenly. Someone on the broken front platform rested a gun barrel on the brake-wheel and fired a quick shot up at Callahan. He heard the sage crackle beside him. Then he watched Marsh Hoagland stand up on the platform and plug another shell into the gun. Hoagland was erect and to the last appeared to command the situation. But he had lost: He could not miss it, Callahan realized. He had been whipped by a stage and six horses. He stood with a bloody face in the bottom of a gully, with escape cut off, with nothing left for him but death.

Callahan rose up. "Give up, Marsh," he called. "You haven't a show of making it."

Hoagland patiently finished loading and raised the

gun, but Callahan's carbine rocked then, spitting a smut of black powder and a ball of molded lead. Hoagland dropped the gun and lurched backward. He was out of their vision. But a boot lay in sight, moving slowly.

The bank books were in the safe. There was forty-six thousand dollars in various savings accounts throughout the Territory of Colorado. The gold was in his money belt and there was a suitcase full of gilt-edged bonds. He had been a frugal man, Marsh Hoagland, except with other people's money.

They dragged blankets from the car and holed up in the brush for the night, mindful of Indians. They lay there thinking of their loves. Gentry voiced his with gentle remembrance.

"She held together, Craig! They hit her full power, but she held. There ain't a nail, nor hardly a screw, in a good stagecoach. Dove-tails and glue! That's the ticket. Pitched that enjine right on its rump in the gully! It was worth losing the coach to see it."

You're getting along, old timer, thought Callahan. A man who could think of anything but women at a time like this was no child.

"There'll be stages in this country as long as we're around," he said. "Rails to the outfitting points, stages to where things are happening. We may find stages are the best part of our business yet! The cream!"